OTHER
Harlequin Romances
by MARY BURCHELL

1029—CHOOSE WHICH YOU WILL
1075—CINDERELLA AFTER MIDNIGHT
1100—THE BROKEN WING
1117—DEARLY BELOVED
1138—LOVING IS GIVING
1165—WARD OF LUCIFER
1187—SWEET ADVENTURE
1214—THE MARSHALL FAMILY
1244—WHEN LOVE IS BLIND
1270—THOUGH WORLDS APART
1298—MISSING FROM HOME
1330—A HOME FOR JOY
1354—WHEN LOVE'S BEGINNING
1382—TO JOURNEY TOGETHER
1405—THE CURTAIN RISES
1431—THE OTHER LINDING GIRL
1455—GIRL WITH A CHALLENGE
1474—MY SISTER CELIA
1508—CHILD OF MUSIC
1543—BUT NOT FOR ME
1567—DO NOT GO, MY LOVE
1587—MUSIC OF THE HEART

MUSIC OF
THE HEART

by

MARY BURCHELL

HARLEQUIN BOOKS   TORONTO
WINNIPEG

Original hard cover edition published in 1972
by Mills & Boon Limited, 17 - 19 Foley Street,
London W1A 1DR, England

© Mary Burchell 1972

Harlequin edition published May, 1972

SBN 373-01587-9

Printed in Canada

1587

CHAPTER ONE

SHE had meant to be at the station in very good time. Dressed with the sort of careless charm which requires considerable forethought, carrying her week-end case with the ease of one who has just stepped from a taxi, presenting her ticket at the barrier with almost offhand casualness, she would be able to greet Oliver Bannister with self-possession and poise.

None of this happened, however. As she emerged from her small flat the heavens opened and the rain came down in torrents. Every taxi was instantly snapped up and there was nothing to do but rush for the nearest Underground station. Her journey involved two changes, each of them with some delay, and by the time she arrived at Victoria there was a long queue of damp or drenched passengers at each booking office window.

Biting her lip with impatience, she inched her way forward, finally snatched her ticket and, with her week-end case – which now felt as though it were loaded with pig-iron – bumping against her legs, she ran helter-skelter for the barrier at which Oliver had promised to meet her.

He was there, anxiously scanning the crowds, and before she could gasp out any word of explanation he seized her case, shoved her unceremoniously before him past the barrier and hustled her along the platform at a brisk trot. As the whistle blew he wrenched open the door of a blessedly uncrowded compartment, and they both almost literally fell in. Even before he had hoisted their luggage on to the rack the train started, and they both collapsed into corner seats and began to laugh.

'I'm terribly sorry! I couldn't get a taxi in that downpour, and it took ages on the Underground.'

'Don't apologize. I was only two and a half minutes before you myself,' he assured her. 'Praying all the way that you'd somehow be later than I was.'

'Honestly?'

'Honestly,' he affirmed. That was one of the nice things about Oliver. He seldom held one to blame for anything. Mostly, she suspected, because he felt equal to any crisis that came along.

No wonder he was popular. So popular that for some time after she first met him at a students' concert she refused to take his advances at all seriously. So many people ran after him that it seemed absurd to suppose that she, the rather unimportant Gail Rostall, should make any special impression.

Indeed, did she even *want* to make a special impression? She was not at all sure about that. For to Gail, after four hard but rewarding years as a singing student, it still seemed that no man – no person, in fact – could be half as important as the career on which she had set her heart.

At first she had taken it for granted that Oliver was no more than just another student, like herself. It was only later that she discovered he had already had some success as a composer of light music.

'Not up your street, I expect,' he had said. 'With your serious little face, your dedicated air and your oratorio type of voice.'

'I'm not so serious!' Gail had protested. 'And although I was more than grateful for my few chances of singing in oratorio, an operatic career is what I've set my heart on.'

'Worse and worse.' He shook his head with a teasing

grin. 'Genuine opera buffs are always the most condescending about my type of tuneful nonsense.'

'I can't afford to be condescending about anything or anyone,' Gail had told him frankly. 'All I can boast of are a few minor engagements. If you have really composed something – *anything* – and had it performed, I'm lost in admiration.'

Oliver Bannister, who seemed to like the idea of her being lost in admiration, said, 'You're a darling. And why haven't I met you before?'

'Probably because we've both been busy in our different fields.'

'I can't imagine being too busy to notice *you*,' he retorted.

And when she asked demurely if he had been getting results with that line, he burst out laughing and said, 'You got that out of an old film.'

'How did you know?' She laughed too.

'Because I went to the same film, I expect. What are you doing on Saturday evening? I have tickets for the National.'

That was the first of several evenings together. But, still with her heart and mind on her work, Gail refused to be stampeded into anything more than a pleasant, casual friendship. He was faintly piqued by this, she saw. But not apparently to the extent of dropping her. On the contrary, he pursued the friendship with something like obstinacy, and finally invited her home for the week-end to meet his family.

'Don't look so dubious,' he said impatiently when he saw her waver. 'Musical people are always coming and going at our place, and my mother makes them all welcome in her slightly theatrical way. It's rather fun, as a matter of fact.'

It sounded fun! Much more fun than a week-end on her own in her minute flat near Hampstead Heath. So she had accepted the invitation. And, since she *had* accepted, she wanted of course to make as pleasing an impression as possible.

But if her careful preparations had gone amiss, he seemed none the less charmed by her slightly storm-tossed appearance now. As he leant across to offer her the afternoon papers, he jerked his head towards the other three passengers and whispered, 'This lot will be getting out at Gatwick, and we'll probably have the place to ourselves after that.'

She smiled non-committally and, accepting one of the proffered newspapers, pretended to become absorbed in it. In reality, she allowed her thoughts to wander over the meeting which lay ahead. For, without seeming actually reticent about his family, Oliver had never, she realized now, referred to them at all until he had thrown out his casual invitation.

'I'll ask him for a few details when we're on our own,' she thought. Then, from force of habit, she turned to the musical page of her paper, to study the news, views and gossip displayed there.

What immediately caught her attention was a paragraph headed, 'Contralto Heroine for New Opera'. As a contralto herself, she had long ago discovered that sopranos have an altogether unfair proportion of the plum roles in opera, and it was with very personal interest that she read on:

'Following on the success in Cologne last year of his sacred cantata "Naomi", Marcus Bannister has turned his hand to opera and has just completed a full-length work entitled "The Exile". I understand that even such seasoned judges as Oscar Warrender and Max Egon have been greatly impressed, which leads one to hope that it will not be too long before we hear this work in London. An interesting feature is that the part of the heroine – described as a strongly dramatic role – is written for a contralto, which makes the casting much more difficult, of course, than if the role were the more usual soprano.'

Dropping the paper in her lap, Gail stared out of the window, distinctly hearing again the words which her teacher had spoken that very week.

'Yours is not a world-shaking organ,' Elsa Marburger had said. 'But it's a voice of quality, and that authentic "brown velvet" type of contralto is rare. So, of course,' she added realistically, 'are the opportunities for using it. Operatically speaking, there are few outstanding roles which require it. Now in oratorio—' And Madame Marburger, who had been a distinguished oratorio singer herself, had left the sentence unfinished.

At that moment the train began to slow down as it neared East Croydon, and Gail glanced down at the newspaper again. As she did so, the name 'Bannister' seemed almost to start out of the paragraph at her. And suddenly, so abruptly that the woman in the far corner glanced up, she said to Oliver,

'Are you any connection of Marcus Bannister?'

'Brother,' replied Oliver briefly. 'Why?'

For answer she silently handed him the newspaper, with the page folded back at the relevant news item.

He skimmed through it so casually that it was obviously no news to him. Then he handed back the paper and said, 'Yes, I know about it, of course. There was a long article about it in the *Telegraph* last week. Didn't you see it?'

She shook her head, and he added, 'You'll be meeting Marc this week-end, if it interests you.'

9

If it *interested* her! How did Oliver suppose it could do anything else? In addition to meeting the composer of a talked-of new opera, she would also, she realized, be meeting perhaps the most distinguished musical family in the country. For if Marcus Bannister – and, to a lesser extent, Oliver – were already making names for themselves, their father, Quentin Bannister, was a figure of international reputation in the musical world. Pianist, conductor, famous for his master-classes and his support of a promising youth orchestra, he was the kind of many-sided genius whose name becomes a household word even among people with little interest in music as such.

Her mind was buzzing with questions she wanted to ask. And when, as Oliver had prophesied, they were left alone in the compartment at Gatwick, she burst out, 'Why did you never *tell* me?'

'Tell you what?' he countered lightly.

'That you're one of *the* Bannisters.'

'I thought you probably knew. Most people do. Anyway—' he laughed – 'perhaps I wanted to be loved for myself alone. There's such a thing as liking to be an individual, you know, instead of the least important member of a family circus.'

It was the half scornful last phrase which gave her the clue that, under all that easy good humour, there was a strain of totally unexpected bitterness.

'But you *are* an individual in your own right, Oliver!' she protested. 'And it's nonsense to speak of yourself as the least important member of – of your family. You've already created music of your own kind. And – who knows? – you may still end up as the most celebrated of the family.'

' "Unexpected triumph of younger son", you mean?' He laughed, his good humour apparently restored.

'Are you very much the younger?' she inquired curiously.

'Six years. I'm twenty-three,' he said, apparently willing to supply information about himself and leave her to do her own bit of mental arithmetic so far as his brother was concerned.

'And there are just the two of you?'

'It's enough.' He made a face. 'With both the parents artists too, there's enough temperament in our household.'

'Then your mother is a musician too?'

'No. A straight actress. She was Daisy Bannister. She and my father were remote cousins, so she didn't have to change her name. She was already part of the charmed circle.' Again that slight curl of his lip that was faintly discontented.

'Daisy Bannister,' Gail repeated thoughtfully. 'The name is familiar, though I can't recall having seen her on the stage.'

'Probably not. She retired a dozen years ago, and you'd only have been a tiddler then. I'm never quite sure why she did retire,' he added reflectively.

'I suppose she preferred family life,' Gail suggested.

'Oh, no!' He laughed immoderately at that suggestion. 'She isn't the least bit domesticated or maternal in the usual sense of the term. In fact, I sometimes think she could only have had Marc and me in a moment of mental aberration. – She's the most beautiful thing I ever saw.' He stated that as a simple fact rather than a filial boast. 'Indeed, my guess is that it was her sheer beauty which pushed her to the top, rather than anything deep or subtle about her acting. When I last saw her on a stage of course I was a bit young to exercise any real judgment. But I seem to remember her as Daisy-Bannister-being-marvellous rather than the actual character. I've even forgotten just who the character was. Significant, isn't it?'

'I suppose it is,' Gail smiled doubtfully.

In no circumstances could she have imagined herself dissecting her own mother in that smiling, critical way. But then of course her mother was not an actress. Indeed, her whole family was blessedly ordinary. Perhaps her father was something of a delightful anachronism, being what one could only describe as the old-style family doctor, while her mother was the affectionate, practical, ever-present centre of the home. So far as Gail could judge she was perfectly satisfied, looking after her busy husband and her two younger children, while her one talented chick trod the difficult path to vocal fame in London.

Suddenly she felt unaccountably homesick. She even found herself wishing that she were going home to her own family in faraway Northumberland, rather than visiting the fascinating but formidable Bannisters. And because there was all at once an irresistible compulsion to speak about them and give them some sense of reality, she said rather huskily, 'My family aren't a bit like yours.'

'My dear, I'm sure of that!' He was both touched and amused by this statement, she saw. 'They can't be anything but delightful if they produced you. Tell me about them.'

So she told him something of her mother and father, and the twins, Veronica and Simon. And in so doing she steadied both her nerves and her voice.

'The twins think I'm famous already, just because I've had a few minor engagements and some kind reviews.' She smiled.

'They're only anticipating things a little,' he declared

confidently. 'You're *going* to be famous – I'm sure of that. Your voice is one of the loveliest I've ever heard, and that's not just prejudice on my part. I'm only sorry your voice is too dark and real for my kind of stuff. It's the genuine article. More up Marc's street, I'd say.'

Then, as the train began to slow down again and he stood up to collect their luggage, he added almost carelessly, 'Maybe you're the girl he's looking for to take the lead in his new opera.'

She felt a sudden constriction of her throat.

'You did say he would be there this week-end, didn't you?' Again her voice was slightly husky, but with excitement this time.

'Oh, I expect so. In fact—' he glanced from the window as they drew into the pretty little station – 'there he is outside in the car. I thought Mother was going to meet us. But she seems to have pressed Marc into service instead.'

They surrendered their tickets to a friendly collector who said, 'Afternoon, Mr. Bannister. Your brother's outside in the car.'

'So I see. No, thanks, George – I can manage the bags. We're only week-ending.'

'Bit about your brother in the paper this afternoon,' George volunteered. 'He's a clever one, he is. But then you're all clever,' he added with splendid impartiality.

'Spare our collective blushes,' replied Oliver, and he led the way out to the rather rakish-looking black car which stood there.

The man who got out of the driving seat was sufficiently like Oliver to be obviously his brother, though everything about him was a little darker and, in some way, more clearly defined, from the thick, almost chestnut-coloured hair to the strong, good bone-structure of the face.

'This is Marc,' observed Oliver as he flung their cases unceremoniously into the boot of the car. 'Gail Rostall,' he added over his shoulder to his brother.

The other man smiled briefly as he took Gail's hand and said, 'Come in front with me. Oliver can cram into the back.'

'I thought Mother was going to fetch us,' remarked Oliver as they got into the car.

'She was. But at the last minute she was asked to deputize for some missing celebrity who was to open the village fête. She couldn't refuse.'

'Why not?' countered Oliver.

'Because, as you very well know, she can't resist being the centre of the scene. Also I suppose they really needed someone.'

Oliver laughed, and his brother said to Gail, 'We're not really being disrespectful, Miss Rostall. We know our mamma's little weaknesses as I don't doubt she knows ours. Have you had much to do with stage people?'

'Not really—' began Gail. But Oliver interrupted quickly,

'She's more or less one herself.'

'Oh, I'm *not*! I'm a singer, Mr. Bannister, but I'm quite small fry yet.'

'She's too modest,' Oliver declared. 'She has a splendid voice, as a matter of fact. Very unusual type. A genuine contralto.'

'You don't say,' replied his brother, with a sort of dry politeness which made Gail feel uncomfortable. Then he changed the subject abruptly by drawing her attention to the first view of the house from the road.

It stood at the top of a heavily wooded hill, honey-coloured stone against the varied green of the trees. And she exclaimed quite sincerely, 'How lovely! Is it very old?'

'Not specially.' Marc Bannister's curtness made her wonder if she had sounded gushing.

'Depends what one means by old,' Oliver interjected from the back. 'It's about a hundred years old, which brings it into a good period of country house architecture. Comfortable without being pretentious and a very pleasant place to live in. Wouldn't you say so, Marc?'

'Yes,' said his brother, and that was all.

They turned then into a steep, winding drive, where the trees grew so thickly that they met overhead, making a sort of deep green tunnel. Most of the fading afternoon light was shut out and, partly because of this, partly because she sensed a sort of cool unfriendliness in the man beside her, Gail felt unaccountably depressed, as though this week-end were not going to be at all the party of pleasure she had once anticipated.

The momentary feeling left her, however, as they emerged into the wide gravel sweep before the house itself, which was even more beautiful at close quarters than it had seemed from the road.

As Oliver helped her out of the car, a door at the top of the short flight of steps opened, and a manservant stood ready to receive them. Oliver kept a friendly, reassuring hand under her elbow as they mounted the steps. But Marc – busy either with the car or the luggage – apparently took no further interest in her arrival.

'Is my mother home yet, Eliot?' Oliver inquired.

'Madam is in the drawing-room,' the man replied.

'Then come along and meet her now,' Oliver said to Gail. And he conducted her towards the back of the house and into the loveliest room she had ever seen.

It was immensely wide, and on the side facing the door

long, beautifully proportioned windows looked out on to a terrace and then on to a wonderful view of rolling, wooded country. It was more an elegant music-room than a conventional drawing-room, with a grand piano at either end and a harp, with a beautifully inlaid frame, in one corner. On the walls were several superb eighteenth-century prints showing groups of people playing chamber music.

Of all this Gail took in no more than a superficial impression in that first moment, her chief interest being naturally for the sole occupant of the room – a tall, graceful woman who turned from one of the windows at their entry, with a movement so flowing, so all-in-one-piece, as Gail put it to herself, that it was a delight to see.

As she came forward to take Gail's hand, Oliver's description of her as the most beautiful thing he had ever seen returned irresistibly. And Gail thought she could not have quarrelled with that claim.

Although she must, Gail knew, be somewhere in her late forties at least, she seemed quite ageless. And if one tried to define her looks she was, in some odd way, almost Edwardian in type. Intensely feminine, unhurriedly graceful and sure in her movements, she had a faintly appealing air which was purely a surface matter. For beneath that engagingly vague exterior was someone, Gail felt certain, who knew exactly what she wanted and also how to get it.

She greeted her young visitor in a cool, beautifully pitched voice, but the handclasp was unexpectedly warm and firm. She retained Gail's hand in hers as she turned to her son to offer a beautiful cheek to kiss and, gazing at her in frank admiration, Gail realized that she was studying her hostess as though she were someone on a stage.

That gleaming dark chestnut hair – the same shade as

that of her elder son – was dressed on top of her head in a sort of coronet, a style which belonged to no special fashion or period and was somehow peculiarly her own. It inescapably suggested queenliness, as did her unhurried, graceful movements. And it occurred to Gail that what she and Oliver were being treated to was a superb performance of a devoted mother welcoming the girl her son had just brought home.

She dismissed the word 'performance' from her mind almost as soon as it formed, feeling it was manifestly unfair to attribute anything in the nature of an act to someone who could smile so sweetly and hold one's hand so warmly. But she thought she understood why both the Bannister sons tended to smile half indulgently when they spoke of their mother.

After a few kind words, Mrs. Bannister herself took Gail upstairs to her room, which looked out over the same splendid view as the drawing-room.

'I hope you will be comfortable, dear.' Her thoughts seemed only half on Gail by now. 'Come down when you feel like it. There will be drinks in the drawing-room any time you like, and a few neighbours usually drop in before dinner. Are you interested in music?'

'I sing,' said Gail diffidently.

'You sing? How interesting,' said Mrs. Bannister as though singing were an unusual form of musical activity. 'Professionally? or just for your own pleasure?'

'I'm in my last year of study, and I've also done a few engagements, mostly in oratorio. But—'

'You must sing to us after dinner,' said Mrs. Bannister, with vague kindliness rather than enthusiasm. Then she went away, leaving Gail with the odd impression that the subject might never be mentioned again.

Well, she had not come there to sing.

Or had she?

It had certainly not been in her mind when she accepted that invitation of Oliver's. But at that time she had had no idea that he was one of *the* Bannisters. Gail was not one to gear all her actions to the one ambitious thought of furthering her career. Some people did just that, she knew. Every contact, every so-called friendship was weighed and used with the one idea in mind. That was not her way, and never could have been. But it would have been disingenuous to pretend she was not aware that the Bannisters were the kind of people who represented powerful influence in the musical world. A word from Quentin Bannister – or, in her own case, perhaps more particularly Marcus Bannister – could not fail to be of immense advantage in any career.

She wished she had not found Marcus Bannister so difficult of approach. After those few first pleasant words of polite welcome there had been no point of contact, nothing of his brother's easy, expansive manner.

'But then one can't say very much on a short drive,' she told herself reassuringly. 'Probably later, when we can talk about the things which really interest us—'

She left it at that. And, having changed into a dress which she hoped was suitable evening wear in the rather stately home of the Bannisters, she surveyed herself in the long mirror. The mirror reflected not only Gail but the room behind her, and she was momentarily a little dismayed by the contrast between the simplicity of the one and the elegance of the other.

But perhaps she was being hyper-critical. It was true that nothing in her appearance matched the subdued luxury of her surroundings, where everything spoke – or discreetly whispered – of money lavishly but discriminatingly spent. But her dress, though unpretentious, was tasteful and becoming and everything about her was well groomed, from her luxuriant auburn hair to her un-eccentric shoes.

'She's a nice *clean* child – which is such a relief nowadays,' she had once heard Madame Marburger say of her. And if this would have been modest praise in other days, the compliment was not without significance in the self-consciously scruffy age in which Gail lived.

On closer inspection, she was pleased to see that the sea-green of her dress brought out unusual greenish lights in her hazel eyes and that, in contrast, her fine clear skin looked a warm, almost creamy colour.

'It will do,' she said aloud, and then she went downstairs with a rather delicious sense of excited anticipation.

Since there seemed no one about to give her any directions, she went straight into the drawing-room. And here she found Marc Bannister at one of the pianos, idly trying out a phrase or two of something she did not recognize.

He got up immediately and came forward, but she said hastily and rather confusedly, 'Please don't let me interrupt you.'

'You don't interrupt me,' he told her. 'I was only doing a sort of musical doodling. What will you have to drink?'

She let him pour her a sherry, sought in her mind for a fruitful topic of conversation, and came up with the subject which was naturally uppermost in her mind.

'I read about your new opera in the train coming down.'

'Did you?' There was nothing conversationally helpful in the cool politeness of that.

'I didn't know anything about it until then,' she went on.

'No?'

She very much disliked the note of frank scepticism in that one monosyllable, and she longed to tell him it was pretty conceited of him to suppose that one *must* have heard of his blessed opera.

Gail sipped her drink nervously. And then, as it became necessary to say *something*, and apparently he thought she ought to know about his opera, she went on with the subject.

'It's an intriguing title,' she ventured. ' "The Exile".'

'That was the librettist, David Eversleigh. I was very fortunate to have such a good librettist.'

This was better. At least he had volunteered a whole statement!

'It's pretty important, isn't it?'

'To have a good librettist? It's vital.' His feelings were evidently so intense on this matter that he became really animated. 'Half the operas written today are just non-starters because of an unprofessional and pretentious libretto. Many of them have the kind of theme that would make quite a good short story or essay. But there is nothing stage-worthy about them at all.'

'You mean—' suddenly she smiled in mischievous agreement – 'the kind of thing which is written up pompously beforehand, "explained" by one involved party or another, and finally given the kiss of death by being described as profoundly interesting and thought-provoking.'

'Exactly.' For the first time he laughed, and she watched with sheer pleasure the way his face and his whole personality seemed to change. 'All very meritorious and unemotional, but it just doesn't add up to an opera.'

'And "The Exile" really is stage-worthy, I take it?'
She looked at him with genuine sympathy and interest.

'I think so. It's always difficult to tell with any piece of
theatre before you've actually got it on to a stage.'

'Is there some probability that it will be produced quite
soon?'

'I hope so.' Somehow he sounded cautious again.

'And the heroine's role is a genuine contralto one?'

'Yes.' He turned away to pour himself a drink, and she
realized they were back to monosyllabic replies.

She wanted to say, 'You needn't be panic-stricken. I'm
not after your silly old heroine's part.'

But of course she could say no such thing. Anyway, it
would not have been entirely true. For while she had in-
itially accepted this week-end invitation in all ignorance –
and innocence – how could she possibly be *indifferent* to
the discovery that she had come to the fountain-head, so
to speak, of a new and already much-discussed opera?

While she was thinking what else she could say without
giving offence, they were interrupted by the entrance of
Oliver. And with him came his father.

Quentin Bannister, then at the height of his fame, was
nothing like so immediately attractive as either his wife
or his sons. A stocky man, with a shock of grey hair, he
looked more like a prosperous farmer than the popular
idea of a musician. But when he spoke Gail discovered
that he had one of the most attractive speaking voices she
had ever heard. He also, she realized almost immediately,
had that elusive gift called star quality. Why she could
not have said, but he instantly and without effort became
the centre of the scene, the director of the conversation,
and the magnet which drew everyone's interest and attention.

He had none of his wife's vagueness, and certainly none

21

of the sceptical wariness which his elder son had displayed. On the contrary, he greeted Gail with, 'Oliver tells me you have a very good contralto voice and that Elsa Marburger thinks well of you. We must hear you later on.'

'Do you know Madame Marburger?' Gail was charmed.

'Of course. Excellent teacher. Had a very serviceable voice herself in her time. I heard her first in "The Kingdom" at the Three Choirs Festival, thirty years or more ago. Took that high entry so well that I thought it must be a fluke at the time. But I heard her do it again on other occasions. It was perfect placement and no fluke. Has she passed on some of her admirable technique to you?'

'I – I should like to think so.' Gail smiled at him.

'Well, so should I. We'll hear for ourselves later on.' Then he turned to his elder son and said, 'That's a stupid bit about you in the evening paper.'

'Which one? They were both kind enough to mention me,' replied Marc imperturbably.

'Were they? I only saw one,' exclaimed Gail, and then blushed at having broken into someone else's conversation.

'Where they quoted you as saying you'd rather not have "The Exile" performed at all than have the wrong vocal colour for the heroine.'

'Well, I didn't actually say that,' Marc replied. 'But it's very nearly true, I suppose.'

'Nonsense.' Quentin Bannister's beautiful voice suddenly became very bracing and forthright. 'No musical work is worth much so long as it exists only on paper.'

'You mean that one should make any sort of compromise just to get a hearing?' his son said disdainfully.

'No, of course not. I mean that only a fool ruins a practical proposition by sticking out for the smallest detail.'

'I don't call the right type of voice for my heroine the smallest detail,' retorted Marc disagreeably.

At which his father said, 'Pshaw!' which delighted Gail who had never heard anyone say that before and, like most of us, had sometimes wondered how it was really pronounced.

'Where's your mother?' Quentin Bannister addressed both his sons impartially. But she answered for herself by coming into the room at that moment, looking strangely like someone out of a fairy tale in a trailing silver-grey dress of indeterminate design.

'I'm here, dear,' she said, in that low, charming voice of hers. But even without her words Gail would have known she was there simply by looking at the change in Quentin Bannister's expression. On to his healthy, strong-featured face had come a slight, wondering smile, and Gail realized that even now, nearly thirty years after he had married her, Daisy Bannister was still the darling, ultimate miracle to her famous husband.

'Put on some more lights, Marc,' she said. 'I think the Forresters have just arrived. And — I forgot to tell you, darling, and I hope you won't mind — they're bringing Lena Dorman with them.'

'I don't mind in the least,' replied Marc, in a tone which meant that he did, Gail could not help thinking.

He put on more lights, however, so that the lovely room sprang into life like a superb stage set. Momentarily, it gave Gail an even more pronounced feeling of taking part in some delightful but improbable play. Then half a dozen newcomers entered the room, to be greeted warmly by the two older Bannisters and with varying degrees of pleasure or mere courtesy by Oliver and his brother.

As is usual on these occasions, Gail failed to register everyone's name. But she identified the Forresters as a pleasant, middle-aged couple – rather unexpected companions for the striking girl who accompanied them.

Lena Dorman – Gail found the name faintly familiar, though she was not sure why – was not strictly beautiful, but there was something arresting about her, partly because of her air of cool confidence which almost demanded attention and interest. No single feature of her face was outstandingly lovely, but she had a wonderful mobility of expression which made it, Gail knew instantly, what one calls 'a stage face'.

She went almost at once to Marc who stood, slightly withdrawn, by one of the pianos.

'Hello, Marc. Congratulations on the new work.'

'Not before it has stood the test of an actual performance,' he replied coolly. 'How's the German scene?'

'Musically speaking, you mean?'

'Of course. Nothing else interests you, does it?'

'No.' There was an odd touch of defiance in her reply. 'For me the German musical scene is fine. I never looked back after the Cologne "Naomi".'

'I believe you,' he said, still in that very cool tone.

Then Gail's attention was claimed by Oliver and she overheard no more of what she felt was an interesting and significant conversation.

'None of them will stay very long,' Oliver told her quietly. 'I hope you're not finding this tiring.'

'Not in the least,' she assured him. 'I'm fascinated. Who is the girl talking to your brother? I caught her name, but I can't quite place her.'

'She's very much an up and coming soprano. Marc chose her himself for his cantata "Naomi" when it had its world premiere in Cologne."'

'And that really launched her?'

'No, I wouldn't say quite that. She was already beginning to make a name for herself. But I suppose it gave her a valuable boost. At any rate, as a result of "Naomi" she got in with one of the big international agents. She's been his white-headed girl ever since.'

'I – see.' Again Gail glanced with interest at the couple by the piano. 'Was your brother rather – sweet on her?' she inquired on impulse.

'I don't think so.' Oliver looked genuinely surprised. 'He's not much interested in anything but his music, you know.'

Then Mrs. Forrester came up and said pleasantly that she had just heard that Gail was a singer and a pupil of Elsa Marburger.

Gail made the usual polite replies to the usual questions, and then asked if Mrs. Forrester were a singer herself.

'Oh, no, my dear! It's shaming to have to admit it in this company, but I don't sing or play a note. My niece—' she nodded in the direction of the two by the piano – 'is the only real performer in our family. But being neighbours of the Bannisters keeps us very much in the musical scene. I can at least claim that I am a devoted and reasonably knowledgeable listener.'

Gail decided that she liked Mrs. Forrester and said, very truly, that no performer, great or small, could afford to underestimate a good listener.

'Well, that's true,' Mrs. Forrester laughed. 'I hope the Bannisters will bring you over to our place some time tomorrow.'

Soon after that the company broke up, and the Bannisters and their house-guest went in to dinner, in a charming, panelled dining-room where the atmosphere was a good deal more intimate than in the big music-room.

Gail was healthily hungry by now. But between Mrs. Bannister's vague reference to her singing, Quentin Bannister's forthright request for it, and Marc's crushing lack of enthusiasm about it, she was still not at all sure whether or not she would be expected to perform later. She felt she must play for safety, however, and so she ate rather sparingly until Oliver asked with some concern, 'Aren't you hungry, Gail?'

'Oh, yes! and I'm enjoying my dinner immensely,' she assured him.

'She's hoping to be asked to sing later,' observed Marc so drily that Gail had some difficulty in resisting a sudden desire to kick his ankle smartly under the table.

'She *is* going to be asked to sing later,' Quentin Bannister stated. 'I am particularly anxious to hear her.' And it was suddenly plain to Gail that, for some reason or other, Quentin Bannister and his elder son had anything but a harmonious relationship.

The last thing she wanted was to be a bone of contention between them. At the same time, she could not help giving the older man a very warm and grateful smile as she remembered his reputation for being specially sympathetic towards young artists.

By the time he brought up the subject again, half an hour or so after they had returned to the music-room, Gail had already decided what she would sing.

'I'd like to do something from Gluck's "Orfeo",' she said, steering a careful path between the twin traps of coy prevarication and over-eagerness to air her gifts.

'Not "Che faro", for pity's sake,' put in Marc dis-

26

agreeably. 'It's every aspiring contralto's party piece.'

'I thought of doing Orpheus's appeal to the Furies,' Gail told him tartly, and Marc's father laughed suddenly.

'Come along,' he said, patting her on the shoulder. 'I'll play for you. And Marc can sit there and glower as one of the Furies, if he likes.'

For a moment Gail thought Marc was going to get up and leave. But then something – perhaps belated regret for his rudeness or perhaps just sheer curiosity – seemed to hold him there. He stirred impatiently in his chair, but at least he remained. His mother went on placidly doing tapestry work, with a concentration which set her slightly apart from the scene. And Oliver was really the only one who leaned forward with any air of eagerness.

But – as she was to remember with surprise afterwards – from the moment Quentin Bannister took her over to the piano, Gail hardly thought of anyone else in the room. To some extent, he was still her kind, well-wishing host, but suddenly he had also become the knowledgeable professional musician who knew exactly how to get the best out of any artist under his direction.

'We'll take it from here—' he indicated a passage in the piano score. 'I'll play these last few pages of the Dance of the Furies so that you get the right atmosphere. Don't bother about this room – or anyone in it. Look out through the windows into the night, and remember you've come to the edge of Hades to plead for the one person you love, and that you have nothing to rely on but your voice and your lyre.'

'I'll remember,' Gail said softly. And she looked out

over the shadowy garden and the hills beyond, while there suddenly poured forth from the piano such a welter of sound and fury that it seemed as though a whole orchestra were playing.

Then suddenly, magically, as the feverish sound died away, there stole over the scene the limpid heavenly notes of a lyre, so exquisitely produced that it seemed impossible that any piano could be sounding them.

Gail was absolutely entranced by the way Quentin Bannister evoked the operatic scene, but the well-schooled, disciplined part of her was sufficiently free of the spell to bring her in at the right moment. She was surprised herself at the beauty and precision of her entry. And then she was aware of something else – the merging of her art with that of a much greater artist. It was exactly as though she and the elderly man at the piano were one force.

She had no idea how he produced his overwhelming effects. But they were all there. The angry cries of the Furies, the plangent phrases of the lyre, the very voices of the raging creatures answering her pleas. And through it all she heard her own voice – as though she could be both listener and performer – weaving the magic thread of sound until its spell was complete, and the chorus of protest and refusal sank at last into a sort of growling submission.

It is, of course, a scene which never fails of its effect. And at the end there was a moment's silence, as though everyone – even Gail herself – were stunned by it. Then Oliver, speaking almost in a whisper, said, 'Gail! I had no idea you could sing like that.'

And Quentin Bannister got up from the piano and said, 'That's a very beautiful voice of yours, my dear. And you use it extremely well.'

'But – *you*!' Gail turned to him with both her hands out. 'You! I never heard anything like it. You created orchestra and stage in one. Like – like a miracle. Like—' and suddenly overcome by her own excited emotions, she put her hands over her face.

'Oh, come, come!' Amused, but undoubtedly pleased, the older man put his arm round her. 'I've been doing this sort of thing a long time, you know. I'm an old hand at it.'

'It's not that.' She dropped her hands and looked at him. 'It's not that at all. I suppose,' she said slowly, 'it's the first time I've experienced real genius at close quarters. It's – it's like an elemental force.'

'Well, I must say you have a nice turn of phrase for flattering an old man,' Quentin Bannister laughed, and actually dropped a light kiss on her hair. 'We must try you out on something else tomorrow. Marc, what about letting her try the first act monologue in "The Exile"? It's an idea.'

'Yes, it's an idea,' replied Marc, in a tone which implied it was not a very good idea.

And then a maid wheeled in a tea trolley, and Mrs. Bannister proceeded to dispense China tea and cold drinks, along with the sort of harmless social conversation which is guaranteed to take the tension out of any situation.

From then until she went to bed Gail had a nice, cosy chat with Oliver in a secluded corner of the music-room, during which he repeated his incredulous delight in the way she had sung, and added, for good measure, that she had obviously made a great hit with his father.

'I said no more than I really felt,' Gail assured him. 'I think he's terrific, don't you?'

'Oh – yes, he's terrific all right.' Oliver grinned good-

29

humouredly. 'It's hard work living in his shadow, though, and he does try to run our lives too, you know. I don't mind it so much, because he doesn't really think I'm sufficiently gifted to warrant much interference. But Marc's a different proposition.'

'They don't get on well, you mean?'

'Well, it's difficult for them both, Marc being a very gifted composer and my father everything *but* that. It just isn't in him, and I think he's never quite resigned himself to the fact. When Marc began to show signs of genuine talent, Father pretty well wanted to take over and tell him what to do. It didn't go down at all well with Marc. He's a lone wolf anyway.'

'I – see. It's tricky, isn't it?'

'Very tricky,' Oliver agreed, but he laughed light-heartedly enough. And rather soon after that she said goodnight, because suddenly she was very tired after the varied experiences of the evening.

Both her host and hostess bade her a kind goodnight, but Marc was nowhere about, so she had to go without speaking to him. When she was half-way up the wide staircase, however, he came out of a room at the side of the hall and stood looking up at her.

'Miss Rostall,' he said quietly, 'there's something I want to say to you.'

'Yes?' She looked over the stair-rail in surprise at him.

'I thought your singing this evening was quite beautiful—'

'*Did* you?' She was indescribably gratified and came several steps down again until she stood only a little way above him.

'—But there's something I want to make quite clear. I have no intention of being stampeded into giving you the leading role in my opera, however much Oliver may push your claims, or you yourself may ingratiate yourself with my father. It will be easier for all of us if you understand that here and now.'

CHAPTER TWO

There was a moment of stunned silence. Then Gail said in a tone of cold fury, 'If this is going to be a moment of truth then let *me* tell *you* that I'm not in the least interested in your silly little opera, hard though you may find it to believe me.'

'As a matter of fact, it isn't either silly or little.' Suddenly he smiled up at her with genuine amusement and a touch of compelling charm she had not suspected in him. 'It's a full-length work and, if I may say so, it's rather good.'

'I don't care what it is. I never heard of it or you before this afternoon and—'

'Didn't you really?' She saw the statement intrigued him and that he was almost tempted to believe her. 'But you must admit it was a singular coincidence, your turning up here, within days of the details of my opera being made public – complete with genuine contralto voice and a great desire to please.'

'There was no desire to please you,' she told him coolly. 'And though this opera may be the highlight of a decade for you, for me it's no more than an untried work that I'm hearing about for the first time. For all I know, it may be dismal.'

'Well, of course that's true,' he admitted, and again that extraordinarily charming smile flitted across his face. 'You have a distinctly deflating turn of phrase, I must say.'

'You asked for it!'

'I suppose I did,' he agreed unexpectedly. 'I'm sorry.'

'Oh—' she was almost completely disarmed. 'I – I'm sorry too. I didn't mean to drub you quite so heartily. But you seemed so convinced from the outset that I was only here to make use of you and—'

She stopped suddenly at the stormy look which came into his face. Then, on an inexplicable impulse, she leaned over the banister and said, quite kindly, 'It was because you *had* been made use of in that way once before, wasn't it?'

'I don't know what you mean.' He looked startled and there was almost a rough note in his voice.

'I mean Lena Dorman,' Gail replied calmly. 'She made up to you because she wanted to sing in the world premiere of your cantata, didn't she? And then, when she'd got what she wanted, she left you flat for someone she thought would be of more use to her.'

'Who told you *that* story?' He narrowed his eyes. 'Oliver?'

'Oh, no. I don't think Oliver knows anything about it.'

'Then what makes you think you do?'

'My excellent powers of observation,' Gail told him coolly. 'And in view of what I saw – and deduced – I forgive you now for all your rudeness and wish you good-night.'

Having said which she turned and went on up the stairs, pleasingly aware that she was making a splendid exit, and that he watched her in silence all the way.

Alone in her own room she found that she was breathless and a good deal shocked by her own bold candour. But there was not a word that she would have retracted and she spent no time lying awake regretting anything that had happened that evening. On the contrary, she fell asleep immediately, slept dreamlessly and awoke to find the late summer sunshine streaming in at the windows of her lovely room.

Even lying in bed she could see across country to the wooded hills beyond. But, entrancing though the distant view might be, she was more interested in what lay near at hand. So she got up and dressed, enjoying to the full her luxurious bathroom – so different from the chilly little slip of a place in her own flat – and then she went down through the silent house and out by a side door.

It was a beautiful morning and all along the terrace the late climbing roses were still in bloom. Their scent was faint and fresh in the morning air, but she guessed that when the sun was on them the terrace would be drenched with their fragrance.

A short flight of steps brought her to the wide lawn and she stood there for some minutes, loving the solitude and the silence. Then Oliver came out by one of the french windows and ran down the steps to join her.

'Hello, you're up early, aren't you?' He stood and smiled at her as though the sight of her there in the grounds of his own home gave him a very special pleasure.

'It all looked so lovely from my bedroom window that I wanted to explore further,' she told him.

'Then come along.' He caught her hand lightly in his. 'I'll take you round.' And they went through the gardens and the orchard together, he quite obviously enjoying her unforced delight in everything that was so familiar to him.

'I'm glad you didn't let Marc's rudeness spoil your pleasure in things,' he said impulsively.

'Oh, that—' She dismissed Marc's rudeness quite lightly, secure in the thought that she had certainly had the last word on the previous evening.

34

'In any case, you know,' Oliver went on, as though he thought she might still need reassuring, 'Father is quite determined that you shall be tried out in this new work of Marc's.'

'But not against your brother's will! I don't think I'd like that,' Gail objected. 'It is *his* opera, after all. He's entitled to cast it his own way.'

Oliver shook his head.

'It's not as simple as that – which is what riles him, I suppose. It isn't an easy matter to get a full-scale work put on the operatic stage unless you have some pretty solid backing – either artistic or financial or both. Marc can have both – in Father. The old man carries a lot of weight in the musical world, both here and abroad. And frankly he is an extremely wealthy man. Marc can't afford to disregard his wishes entirely. Not if he wants his support, that is. And without it his chances of seeing his opera on the stage would be immeasurably reduced.'

'Your father is really as influential as that?' Gail looked dubiously at Oliver.

'Oh, yes. He might very well conduct the work himself.'

'Not Marc?' There was a note of protest in her voice.

'Not very likely. Although he is a more than competent conductor his name wouldn't fill the house, whereas Father's would, of course. These are all things which have to be taken into consideration.'

'But then surely the same thing applies to the casting of the principal roles,' Gail said quickly. 'Which definitely rules me out, however good an impression I might make at an audition.'

'No, it's not quite the same thing,' Oliver told her. 'There are three major roles – the other two being for mèn. If both these were taken by established artists one

35

could risk a really promising unknown for the girl. Indeed, it would add an element of interest and piquancy if one did so. I have an idea that's what is in Father's mind.'

'You *have* got it all worked out, haven't you?' She smiled at him, but her sense of excitement began to mount once more.

'Of course. Little else has been talked of in the family for months.' Oliver shrugged expressively. 'It's only recently that the whole thing became public. But here, at home—!' He laughed. 'One doesn't have a new opera every day, even in the Bannister family.'

'Oliver—' she turned and faced him – 'was all this in your mind when you invited me down here?'

'Most of it.' He smiled back at her. 'I like you, Gail. You may have noticed that. And I like your voice. I don't know if it's ideal for the part, but I would have said you had an interesting outside chance. So why shouldn't I arrange that you should have an opportunity to be heard?'

'You're a dear.' She put out her hand and touched his. 'I'm infinitely grateful, and of course the very thought of being considered is intoxicating. But I shouldn't like to – well, to be the cause of any family friction, you know.'

'There's always friction between Marc and Father, whether you're concerned or not,' Oliver told her philosophically. 'A bit more or less won't tear the family apart. In any case, my dear, no one gets to the top of the tree by considering everyone else's sensitive feelings. You must learn to be more thick-skinned about people's likes and dislikes. If you landed this part – and it's a big "if" – it would be a very fine operatic plum for a beginner. Well worth bulldozing through any objections of Marc's, I'd say.'

She winced slightly at the expression. But before she could say any more there was the sound of a distant bell and Oliver remarked with satisfaction,

'That sounds like breakfast, and I for one am ready for it.'

Gail found she was too, and they went into the house together.

For a while they were the only ones in the breakfast room, as they helped themselves from a selection of dishes on an electric hot-plate and from vacuum jugs of coffee and milk.

'There are no hard and fast rules about Sunday breakfast,' Oliver explained. 'Father's a bit of a martinet during the rest of the week, but we all relax on Sundays. Mother usually breakfasts in her room—'

'But not today, dear,' said his mother, coming in at that moment. 'I want to see something of Gail while she is here.' And she smiled kindly at her young guest, who smiled shyly in return.

'When are Marc and my husband going to try you out in this new work of Marc's?' she inquired rather absently, as she helped herself to coffee and paused to put some bread in the toaster.

'I – I don't know,' stammered Gail, a little taken aback, for Mrs. Bannister had shown no special interest in her singing until then. 'I'm not even sure that I'm going to *be* tried out.'

'Why, of course you are. Quentin said so,' replied her hostess simply.

'Perhaps,' Gail suggested diffidently, 'Marc—' she didn't see what else she could call him – 'would prefer not to bother with a beginner like me.'

'Why not?' Marc's mother looked genuinely surprised and, as her elder son came in at that moment she said, with a frankness that made Gail wince, 'What's this about your not wanting Gail to be tried out in something from "The Exile"?'

'I don't know.' Marc dropped a cool kiss on his mother's cheek in passing. 'You tell me.'

'She seems to think you might not like the idea. She's shy about it or something.'

'You surprise me,' said Marc, going over to the sideboard.

'There you are, dear.' Mrs. Bannister smiled reassuringly at Gail. 'You see Marc does want to hear you, after all.'

Gail simply did not know what to reply to this. She longed to explain to Marc that she had not been beating up further family support against him. But there was absolutely no way of doing this without labouring the point insufferably, so she remained uncomfortably silent, aware that her slightly heightened colour did nothing to establish her innocence.

Having helped himself to breakfast, he came and sat down beside her, somewhat to her dismay. But he merely inquired politely if she had slept well, and then if she had any plans for the morning.

'Not – really.' She glanced across at Oliver, but his mother was engaging his attention at that moment.

'Well, come along to the music-room in half an hour,' Marc said, more as an order than a suggestion. 'I'll tell you something of the dramatic situation of the first act and let you have a look at the score beforehand. Then Father and I will hear what you can do.'

'But—' she swallowed slightly – 'I thought you didn't want to hear me in any work of yours.'

'I don't specially,' he replied with brutal indifference. 'But family pressure being what it is, the sooner we get this over the better.'

'Thank you,' she said quietly. 'But I think I'd rather not.'

'Don't be silly. If you reserve the right to get offended over every harsh word that's said to you, you won't get very far in your chosen profession. Take the chance while it's offered—'

'Were you offering me some sort of chance in those few well-chosen words?' she inquired drily. And at that he laughed, and once more she was very much aware of that unexpected, compelling charm.

'Everything represents a chance if you can make some-one listen to you,' he told her grimly. 'It's too early yet to expect composers to go on their bended knee to you. One day they may, and you can then make your own terms, rejecting this and graciously accepting that. But not yet, my dear, not yet. You've a long way to go. Take the rough with the smooth, for I can assure you there's a great deal of rough in the early days of anything that's worthwhile.'

She knew this was all too true. She knew he was in a position to be thoroughly horrid to her and was indulging himself to the full. But she also knew that very few people had the chance of singing to either Quentin Bannister or Marc Bannister, and still fewer had even the remotest chance of being considered by either for an important role in a new and much discussed work.

So she swallowed her chagrin and said, 'Very well. I accept what you say. And – and I'll be glad to sing to you and your father if you'll give me the opportunity.'

'Fine.' He gave her a nod of unmistakable dismissal and turned once more to his breakfast. And Gail, determined to use the half hour profitably, slipped away to her own room where she did some quiet vocalizing, in the hope

39

that both she and her voice would be in a calm and confident condition by the time she faced the proposed opportunity – or ordeal.

When she came down once more and into the music-room, she found Marc already there, sitting at the piano. And he immediately pulled up a chair beside him and said, 'Come over here and I'll explain one or two things.'

She came at once and as she sat down he asked abruptly, 'Are you a good sight-reader?'

'Moderately so.'

In point of fact Gail was an exceptionally good sight-reader, but she was not going to make any exaggerated claims which she might not be able to fulfil.

'Please tell me first something about the dramatic content of the work,' she said. 'Not just the first act, as you suggested, but the whole work. Otherwise I can't think myself into the character of the girl.'

He gave her a glance of something like approval at that, but made no comment. Instead he plunged into a rapid sketch of the story.

'It concerns a small group of people who have left their country by choice, facing incredible hardship and danger, with the idea of seeking freedom in place of tyranny—'

'Then it's a modern scene?' Gail interrupted.

'It is of this century – yes; though it could belong to almost any time in the last hundred years. For throughout that time, as you know, people have been driven into literal or spiritual exile in the name of one horrible tyranny or another. The hero has his scale of values clear, his hopes well defined, and he hás absolutely no regrets for the country he has left behind. To him his flight represented escape, to a country where he could live and breathe and make his future his own way. With the girl, Anya, the issues are nothing like so clear.'

'She has come because of him, of course?'

'Yes. She loves him and has left everything that was familiar and dear to her, just to be with him. For her, freedom is more a word than a way of life. The high-sounding principles of her lover and his friends provide no real comfort for her. She came simply because if she had stayed behind she would have lost him.'

'And so she does have regrets for the past?'

'Yes, of course. She longs for the little simple, familiar things which have made up her life. She is heart-breakingly homesick, but she must hide the fact from the others, because to them it would be ridiculous and shameful even to query the incredibly good fortune which has brought them out of tyranny into freedom. Only one person understands something of how she feels. And that is a youth in the party who has suffered most back in his own country. Because of his experiences he is even a little simple-minded. But he is without rancour or bitterness, almost childlike in his innocence and his shining capacity to be happy on almost nothing.

'The others are impatient with him and treat him more or less as a simpleton. But Anya and he find some comfort in each other because both, for different reasons, remember the old life with affection. He because he always forgets the bad and remembers the good, she because she is utterly homesick.

'It is only when she is alone – or with him – that she can voice her longing for what she has left behind. She still loves her man. He represents everything that is big and strong and wonderful. Given the choice again, she would still have chosen to go with him. But she sings of her homeland when she is alone, for to her it is still inexpressibly dear, even though to most people it would be viewed with horror and distaste. This is what the music – and the singer – should convey.'

'And this is what you want me to try out?'

'No, my dear. This is what my father wants you to try out.'

'You are a beast, aren't you?' said Gail conversationally. 'May I see the score, please?'

He handed it over without a word, perhaps slightly taken aback by her candour. And for a minute or two Gail studied the pages and hummed a phrase or two under her breath. Then she looked up and said, 'Tell me what happens later?' just as though she had not flung that insult at him.

'The inevitable. He falls in love with another girl. A girl who entirely represents the new country he has also fallen in love with. He has no more use for Anya. She is almost a reproach to him in his brave new world, because everything about her is reminiscent of what he has gladly left behind. She clings lovingly to the past, while he looks eagerly to the future. There is, of course, a big scene where he finally rejects her and goes off with the other girl.'

'And then?' Without knowing it, Gail actually sounded anxious – deeply involved – as though the girl were already in some way herself.

'She comes back to the communal house they all shared in the early days, and the boy comes in with the homely request that she will sew a button on his shirt. She breaks down and tells him that her life is in ruins. She can never go back to the country she knew and loved, and for her there will never be a place in this new country. She is the eternal exile.'

'And has he any comfort to offer her?'

'Only the essential wisdom of the simple-minded and

the good in heart. He tells her that no one is an exile except by their own conviction, because all people are needed by each other – if only for so small a thing as sewing on a button. He tells her to look for the light because, however small it is, she will not then see the darkness, and he begins to sing to her one of the simplest of the folk songs from their homeland. And after a minute or two she picks up the shirt and begins to sew on the button, and she joins in the song as the curtain falls.'

'Why, it's a lovely ending!' exclaimed Gail. 'You didn't think of it yourself, surely?'

'Why not?' he looked amused.

'Well, I shouldn't have said you – you—' she stopped, embarrassed by what she had been about to say. But he completed the sentence for her.

'You wouldn't have said I had the heart or imagination for it?'

'That was in my mind,' she admitted.

'Well, I'm not entirely responsible for that last scene. David Eversleigh, the librettist, had more to do with that. The central situation was mine, but we talked it over together many times, of course, before we arrived at what we both wanted.'

'If the music is worthy of the last scene—' began Gail. And then Quentin Bannister came in and, to her surprise, he said without hesitation,

'Oh, it is, it is. It's the best thing Marc's ever done. It takes you by the throat, in the way a last scene should.'

'Thank you.' Marc looked grimly amused and somewhat surprised, but Gail thought he was a good deal pleased.

'Well,' the older Bannister said, 'the line between pure gold and pure corn is perilously thin in any form of art. If you can tread it successfully, you're home and dry so far as the public is concerned, and at least two thirds of the critics will be with you. The other third won't matter, because their praise is the kiss of death anyway. Come on, Gail, let's see what you make of this first act monologue. Are you a good sight-reader?'

'She says – moderately,' interjected Marc on her behalf.

'Well, she's got to be better than moderately good to make the right impression. I'll play it over first – and you listen attentively.'

Gail stood beside him, following so closely that before the first page was completed she was already singing under her breath.

'All right – read it straight off,' the older Bannister told her, and he went back to the beginning.

She sang it through, accurately and well, following quite easily the occasional direction that he gave her. Then at the end she said, 'May I do it again, please? keeping in mind just how she is feeling.'

By now she had the musical shape of the monologue. What she wanted was to show that she had taken the measure of the character and the situation. She stood there for a moment, deep in thought, trying to imagine herself in a foreign country with no chance of ever returning home or even glimpsing the family she loved. Although the situation was entirely theoretical she found herself unbearably moved by it, and presently she just nodded to Quentin Bannister to indicate that she was ready to begin.

But suddenly there was a great lump in her throat and she stopped and gulped and was unable to produce a note.

'What's the matter?' the older man looked up and frowned.

'She's overcome by my music, I hope.' Marc gave that flashing smile.

'N-not only that. It's the situation,' Gail explained. And then, as though she could not help it – 'I was trying to think how I would feel if I could never see my home or my family again, and it – it was a bit too much for me.'

'Don't be ridiculous,' said the elder Bannister with unexpected impatience. 'You should never let your emotions interfere with your art. They're there to serve it, not smother it.'

'Don't bully her,' cut in Marc, equally unexpectedly. 'She's doing her best.'

'Her best isn't good enough if it stops her singing,' growled his father in return. 'Come on, Gail. Stop snivelling and start again.'

So Gail started again. And this time she did manage to convey in the tone of her voice something of the pathos of the words and music, while at the same time allowing her admirable technique to take her safely over the emotional pitfalls. She felt she was giving only half of what she would have liked to express. But at the end the elder Bannister turned from the piano and said to Marc,

'She's good, you know. And the colour of the voice is just right.'

'Yes,' agreed Marc slowly, 'the colour is exactly what I had in mind. And she's musical too. But—' he spoke exactly as though Gail were not there or were stone deaf – 'I doubt if she has the emotional depths for the part.'

'You said I was *too* emotional a few minutes ago,' objected Gail rather indignantly.

'No, I didn't. I said you were doing your best,' Marc reminded her drily. 'It was my father who warned you against sobbing all over the place. But that isn't what I mean. It's not a question of musical expression exactly.

It's – well, I suppose it's an inner knowledge of what suffering really is. You give an acceptable touch of pathos—'

'And absolute pathos is a very rare gift,' put in his father.

'Yes, I know. But it's not enough in this case,' Marc said quickly.

'Well – I don't know—' Quentin Bannister pulled his underlip thoughtfully – 'there's a sort of basic simplicity about Anya. And I'd say this girl has the same quality.' He also spoke as though Gail were deaf or not there, and for quite some minutes they went on discussing her performance in candid detail until she said diffidently,

'Would you rather I went?'

'No. Why?' Quentin Bannister looked surprised. 'I thought you were going to try something from the last act.'

'I'd like to,' Gail admitted. 'But I thought maybe you wanted to talk things over in private, without me there.'

'Nothing is ever talked over in private in this house,' Marc told her disagreeably. 'Everyone volunteers an opinion at the drop of a hat. Apart from which, the Bannisters tend to like living in a sort of showcase. They adore being noticed.'

'I don't know what you're talking about, and I'm not sure that you do either,' exclaimed his father, going an angry brick-red. Then he turned back to the piano, struck a violent chord or two and said impatiently to Gail, 'The very last scene. And Marc can put his undistinguished tenor voice to the service of the boy's part. Come on.'

They both obeyed him unquestioningly, Marc providing his part of the musical dialogue in an agreeable light tenor which had, as his father said, no special distinction about it. But he sang the beautiful final folklike tune with unexpected feeling, and Gail found herself joining in with real artistic pleasure.

'It's absolutely lovely,' she exclaimed involuntarily at the end. 'Whoever sings the part is going to have a wonderful time. I wish it could be me. But I can't think I'm either gifted or experienced enough for it. I'm grateful, though, to have had even the chance of trying it through. I do hope it will be an enormous success, Marc.'

'Why – thank you.' He looked taken aback for a moment. And then, almost as impulsively as she had spoken, he added, 'And don't think you have been absolutely written off. No decisions have been made yet.'

Gail was speechless with astonishment and pleasure. A few words of encouragement from the elder Bannister would not have surprised her. But she had supposed that Marc had rejected her in his own mind from the very beginning.

As it was, his father got up from the piano and said, 'Well, these are early days yet. A great many things have to be discussed before any decisions are made. But we shall keep you in mind, Gail. Now run along and enjoy yourself with Oliver. He probably thinks we have appropriated you for long enough.'

So she went away and found Oliver, out on the terrace. He made no complaint about her having been appropriated by his father and brother. On the contrary, he inquired with genuine enthusiasm how she had got on at the impromptu audition.

'I hardly know,' she said slowly. 'Both of them said I was not entirely out of the running. Perhaps they were just being polite, of course, but—'

'Good lord, no!' Oliver laughed that notion to scorn. 'Neither of them would dream of being polite over anything so important. More likely to be crushingly impolite. They both believe in speaking their minds – and rightly so, I think – over anything to do with their profession. If they say you are still in the running for the part, that's exactly what you are. No more and no less. And frankly, Gail, that's as much as I dared to hope at this stage.'

'It's much, much more than anything I dared to hope!' Gail also laughed, but in sheer delight, and she clasped both her hands round his arm in excited joy and gratitude. 'I could never even have dreamed of such a thing. To be seriously considered for an important role in a new work, even at a hundred-to-one chance—'

'I think you might shorten the odds a little,' Oliver told her amusedly. 'There aren't likely to be ninety-nine other talented contraltos milling around, I assure you. And even if there were—'

'Don't raise my hopes,' she interrupted earnestly. 'I'm trying so hard to keep my feet on the ground. It's better that I should go on thinking how *unlikely* it is that I should be seriously considered. Then I shan't be too disappointed.'

'All right,' he laughed, 'we'll leave the subject for the time being. What would you like to do now? Go for a drive? or just sit about on the terrace and talk about our interesting selves – or what?'

What she really wanted to do was to go away by herself and think and think about the extraordinary scene which had taken place in the music-room. But it would have been both ungracious and ungrateful to say so. Instead, she gladly agreed to sit on the terrace in the sunshine and – in return for the helpful interest Oliver had shown in her affairs – she made him talk a little about his own work.

'Oh, it doesn't really count, in the rarified atmosphere

of the Bannister household,' he declared lightly.

But Gail would not have that. And presently he was telling her about a friend of his who wrote extremely witty lyrics, and how he and Oliver planned to try their hand at sophisticated revue.

'I haven't told anyone else, of course,' he said quickly. 'And it may not come to anything. I mean – we may not be half as bright as we think we are! But it's an interesting idea.'

'It's a splendid idea,' Gail told him firmly. 'And you know – sometimes I have hunches about things, Oliver – and I've a hunch you're going to be very successful over this.'

'Darling girl! Cross my palm with silver and say that again,' he said with a laugh. But he leaned over suddenly and kissed her cheek. And because she felt he had done more for her in the last twenty-four hours than anyone else in half a lifetime, she kissed him lightly in return.

Before they could say anything else – and a little to Gail's discomfiture – Mrs. Bannister came out on to the terrace then to ask if they would like to go over to see the Forresters before lunch.

'Mamie Forrester thought you might like to see their house, Gail. It's much older than this one and very attractive. She rang up just now to suggest it and said she mentioned something of the sort to you yesterday.'

'Yes, she did, and I'd love to go,' Gail said quickly, wondering at the same time if her hostess had seen that light exchange of kisses.

'Then I'll drive you over. Are you coming too, Oliver?'

'Of course,' said Oliver, getting to his feet.

'Your father is busy about some affair of his own. And Marc—' Mrs. Bannister went to the open french windows of the music-room and called – 'Marc, I'm running Gail over to the Forresters' place. I don't expect you want to come?'

The question hung in the atmosphere with just a shade too much meaning, Gail could not help thinking. Then Marc's voice replied coolly,

'Yes, I'll come. Would you like me to drive?'

So in the end the four of them went, Marc driving, as he had suggested, with his mother beside him in the front seat and Gail and Oliver behind.

Most of the way Oliver chatted to Gail, either pointing out places of interest or amusingly recalling incidents from his childhood and boyhood connected with the district. In consequence she heard little of what was being discussed in front. Only once her ear caught the name 'Lena Dorman', pronounced by her hostess in slightly over-tactful tones. And then Marc gave that short laugh of his and said,

'Don't waste so much tact on dead issues, Mother.'

Quite shamelessly, Gail would like to have heard more, even though she knew it was not her business. But just then they turned into a short, straight drive and before them lay a small, but beautifully proportioned Elizabethan house.

'It's been a good deal restored.' Mrs. Bannister turned to speak to Gail. 'But it's been done with perfect taste.'

Gail said truly that she had never seen anything more attractive. And even as she gazed in delight at the house, the front door opened and Mrs. Forrester came out, accompanied by a couple of dogs, who barked vociferously and made a great show of warning off all comers, until Oliver said good-humouredly,

'Shut up, idiots! No need to treat us like strangers. We're all more or less family.'

The description was not lost on Gail, and she was touched and pleased to be included thus. Indeed, within seconds, even the dogs, sniffing agreeably around her, seemed to be accepting her at Oliver's valuation.

Having welcomed them kindly, Mrs. Forrester led the way into a beautiful panelled room, where deep mullioned windows looked out on to a garden. Not such a large or impressive garden as at the Bannisters' home, but most exquisitely in period and in keeping with the house.

Entranced by the riot of colour in the long old-fashioned flower-border immediately outside, Gail went to stand for a minute in one of the windowed embrasures. So she missed the exact moment when Lena Dorman entered. But when she turned back again into the room the attractive, faintly disturbing girl was already there and gravitating apparently quite inevitably to Marc's side.

This time, however, Marc seemed unwilling that they should have any sort of tête-à-tête. Somewhat to Gail's surprise, he turned to include her in the conversation.

'You met Miss Rostall yesterday, didn't you?' he said to Lena.

'Did I? Oh, yes – briefly.' The other girl smiled faintly, though her curiously long, attractive eyes remained entirely untouched by the smile, Gail noticed. 'My aunt was telling me that you too are a singer.'

'I'm not very much more than a student,' Gail admitted.

'Well, we all have to start as students.' The words in themselves were quite unexceptionable, but the tone suggested inescapably that some people never got any further than being students.

Gail found herself flushing slightly. And when the other girl asked carelessly what her voice was, she replied curtly, 'I'm a contralto,' and offered no further information.

'A contralto?' Lena Dorman repeated. And then, with a slight laugh, 'A *contralto*? Just what Marc needs for his new opera, according to all the newspaper reports. Isn't that so, Marc?'

'It is,' he agreed coolly.

'And with all speed Miss – Rostall arrives on the scene?' she laughed again, that very slight, oddly significant laugh. 'So now, Marc, perhaps you'll admit that I'm not the only self-seeking pebble on the beach. It isn't only the conscienceless Lena Dorman who uses her friends to further her career.'

'I assure you—' began Gail angrily. But she was silenced by the sudden grip of Marc's fingers on her arm.

'You do Miss Rostall an injustice,' she was staggered to hear him say. 'As a matter of fact, she came down here at the express invitation of my father and myself. We were both anxious to hear her in the part of Anya. And I might say that we are very much impressed. Very much impressed indeed.'

CHAPTER THREE

GAIL was speechless with astonishment at Marc's sudden defence of her. A defence which even included a flat lie. But her silence was probably the best thing she could have contributed to the conversation at that moment. For, combined with her composed air, it inevitably conveyed the impression that she felt innocent enough to disregard further argument.

Lena Dorman gave that slight laugh once more, but it was not such a scornful laugh this time. It was even, Gail thought, a trifle disconcerted. And she seemed glad that the conversation now became general, so that she could withdraw quite naturally from the awkward three-cornered conversation which had turned so unmistakably against her.

Presently they all drifted out into the lovely garden, and Gail then snatched the chance to speak to Marc quietly.

'Why did you tell that fib about you and your father having invited me down here expressly to hear me sing?' she demanded.

He frowned and looked for a moment as though he were not going to reply. Then he said, not very informatively, 'It seemed the best thing to say in the circumstances.'

'That doesn't answer my question! *Why* did it seem the best thing to say?'

'Nothing else would have convinced Lena that you were innocent of any ulterior motive in coming down here.'

'Did that matter?'

'Yes, I think it did.'

'Even though you yourself were just as suspicious until about ten minutes ago?'

'Until about an hour ago,' he amended.

Gail drew her brows together in a puzzled little frown.

'What happened an hour ago that made you change your mind about me?' she asked.

'Something you said. But never mind that now. You've asked enough questions.' He spoke as though she were a rather tiresome child. 'In any case, the misstatement was not entirely on your account. It was time Lena was slightly deflated. She's a completely self-seeking young woman, and would like to establish that you are the same.'

'That *I* am? But she never met me before this weekend. What has she got against me?'

'Nothing against you personally. You were just the yardstick by which she wanted to measure her own conduct and not find it anything but the general rule.'

'Oh—' For the first time Gail wondered if she had been mistaken in thinking Marc had once been in love with this girl. His lightly contemptuous tone hardly suggested devotion. But then she noticed that his glance followed Lena with a sort of angry – almost hungry – attention which was the very reverse of indifference.

'Well, thank you for defending the purity of my motives,' she said, speaking lightly in her turn. 'And thank you also for deciding to believe in it yourself.'

He transferred his glance to her then and laughed, his whole air suddenly much more relaxed.

'You're a nice kid,' he said unexpectedly. 'And if I overstated our interest in you to Lena, believe me, my father and I were not at all unimpressed by your gifts.'

'Thank you,' Gail smiled. For she knew that praise from that quarter, even if rather negative, was not to be despised. If she carried nothing more than that away with her from the week-end with the Bannisters she might, she decided, be very well satisfied.

The rest of the visit, though pleasant, was artistically uneventful. Guests came in on the Sunday evening, but although there was a good deal of extremely interesting musical discussion – in which Quentin Bannister unerringly took the lead – nothing more was said about Gail or her particular gifts.

As Oliver and she had to catch quite an early train on Monday morning, her host and hostess said good-bye to her overnight.

'Come again, dear. It was delightful to see you,' said Mrs. Bannister kindly. But it was difficult to tell from her charmingly vague air whether she really meant this or whether it was merely her standard farewell to any guest.

Her husband was more forthright.

'I shall have a word about you with Elsa Marburger,' he informed Gail. 'If your further development is interesting, I shall want to hear more of you.'

Gail smiled and flushed with pleasure.

'And whether you do that or not I shall never forget the magic of hearing you recreate the Furies Scene from "Orpheus",' she replied sincerely.

He pinched her cheek at that – an outdated gesture which seemed not only natural to him but entirely charming.

Marc was nowhere about when she went to bed, for which she was genuinely sorry. She would have liked to say good-bye to him. But, to her surprise, he came into the breakfast-room the following morning, just as she and Oliver were hastily swallowing the last of their coffee and toast.

She was not the only one to be surprised at Marc's appearance.

'What got *you* up so early?' Oliver wanted to know. 'I hardly expected you to join in the dawn chorus.'

'I came down to say good-bye to Gail,' was the cool reply. 'Give me your phone number, Gail, in case anything comes up with regard to "The Exile".'

'You – you mean—' she stammered, hardly daring to complete the sentence.

'I don't necessarily mean anything,' he returned rather disagreeably. 'I just want to know where one can get hold of you in the unlikely event of our wanting to contact you further.'

She gave him the number, trying not to look chastened by his words, nor unduly excited still by their implication. And Marc wrote down the number in his diary, while his brother looked on with a certain degree of annoyance as well as amusement. However, since it had been his declared hope that Gail might just conceivably be considered for a role in Marc's opera, he could hardly resent the fact that his brother apparently meant to keep in touch with her.

Later, in the train on the way to town, he warned her not to attach too much importance to the incident of the telephone number.

'Father and Marc will ruthlessly pursue every possible line, and quite as ruthlessly eliminate people later, without regard to any fond hopes they may have aroused.'

'I'm not counting on anything,' Gail assured him. 'I'm just stunned to think that anyone in the Bannister family should want to retain even a faint recollection of me.'

'What about me?' he grinned.

'Oh, you're different! You're Oliver – and my very good friend. It's only with an effort, even now, that I think of you as one of the Bannisters. Do you mind?'

'On the contrary, I'm delighted.' He put his hand round her arm and for a moment she felt the affectionate pressure of his fingers. She remembered again what he had said about longing to be an individual, rather than just a member of a distinguished family. And she liked him all the better for it.

During the next week Gail plunged back into hard work and tried not to indulge in too many dreams. She had one or two minor engagements ahead of her – mostly solo performances with church choirs – and these entailed some extra lessons and some very intensive work.

When she came to one of these lessons late in the week, she found her teacher in a much more talkative mood than was usual with her. She regarded Gail with more than customary interest and said, 'I hear that you sang for Quentin Bannister recently.'

'Yes – I did. Quite informally. In his own house,' Gail explained. 'I didn't mention it because there was nothing professional about it. I – I happened to be a house guest, and the opportunity came up.'

'So he tells me.' Elsa Marburger picked up a letter from her desk. 'Did he give you any opinion?'

'He liked my voice, I think. And he said I had been very well taught—' Gail smiled at her teacher, of whom she was genuinely fond. 'He remembered your singing in "The Kingdom" as long as thirty years ago, so you must have made a great impression.'

Madame Marburger was no more conceited than any good artist should be, but she gave a pleased little laugh at that.

57

'He writes about you with what appears to be genuine interest. He even –' she referred to the letter again – 'ventures to make a few observations about your future development, which I naturally would not ignore from such a quarter. But he writes of you as though he sees you as an operatic artist rather than an oratorio singer.'

'I suppose I gave him the impression that that was my ultimate ambition,' Gail admitted. 'They – the whole family, I mean – were a good deal excited about the opera which his eldest son had just completed and—'

' "The Exile". I read about it,' Madame Marburger put in.

'Yes, that's it. They let me see the score. And Mr. Bannister – both Mr. Marc Bannister and his father – tried me out in some of it.'

'Indeed?' Amusement and a sort of surprised respect showed in her teacher's face. 'With what result?'

'They both said I was not absolutely impossible,' said Gail frankly, and at that her teacher laughed.

'Well, come! they didn't try to turn your head, it seems.'

'Oh, no! There was some very plain speaking.' Gail laughed in her turn, but without rancour. 'I didn't mind. I was just thrilled at such people listening to me at all.'

The older woman gave her a half affectionate glance.

'What is the work like? If it's in a very modern idiom, I shouldn't wish you to try to handle it at this stage.'

'I wouldn't call it modern in the extreme sense,' Gail said thoughtfully. 'It's eminently singable—'

'Well, that's a change,' commented Madame Marburger cynically.

'It has an extraordinarily attractive story – libretto.'

'Tell me about it. I have an extra hour this afternoon,

and I think this merits some discussion before you have your lesson.'

So Gail sat down and, as accurately as she could recall Marc's own words, she told the story of 'The Exile'.

At the end, Madame Marburger simply asked, 'Did anyone comment on your capacity to portray such a character?'

'Yes.' Gail was struck that she should instantly put her finger on what Marc had regarded as the weak spot. 'Marc – Mr. Marc Bannister – said he doubted if I had had enough experience of real suffering to give all the part of Anya. I'm not sure that I know quite what he meant.'

'No?' The older woman looked almost sombrely at the bright face of her pupil for a moment. Then she said a strange thing. 'Happy English child—' she spoke half to herself – 'how should you know how an exile feels? With your long, safe roots in a land that hasn't known conquest for close on a thousand years.'

Gail caught her breath, and for a moment she seemed to glimpse something far beyond the limits of her natural experience. She knew that Elsa Marburger's people were Jewish refugees who had come to England in the troubled days of the nineteen-thirties. But she had never thought much about what that meant. Still less had she ever thought about her teacher as anything but a sensitive artist and an extremely successful woman.

'You mean,' she said slowly, and with a slightly crest-fallen air, 'that I've always been too happy and secure to know or understand how to portray the sort of desolation Anya feels?'

'Not necessarily.' Madame Marburger smiled and even touched Gail's cheek lightly, a rare sign of intimacy from her. 'We don't always have to have experienced something in order to portray it, thank heaven. Sensitivity and a sympathetic heart – and you have both – can often give one the clue. And you have a natural gift for pathos which—'

'Mr. Bannister said that!' interrupted Gail eagerly. 'Mr. Quentin Bannister, I mean. And he said it was a rare gift.'

'Well, it is.' Madame Marburger was not displeased to find herself in agreement with him over this.

'Does he—' Gail glanced eagerly at the letter which her teacher was still holding – 'does he mention anything about the opera?'

'Nothing. He states a general interest in your development, and says that some time when he is in London he would like to hear you again. Preferably during a lesson.'

'And you would be willing for him to do that?'

'Certainly. It's an unusual request – if request is quite the word,' she added a little drily as she looked back at the letter and obviously took in its terms afresh. 'I don't want to raise undue hopes, Gail. But it certainly looks as though you've aroused a most useful degree of interest in someone who could do a great deal for your career. And now we'll begin the lesson.'

So the lesson was begun after that and took its customary course. Gail kept her thoughts as far as possible on what she was doing and not until the end did she venture to ask the question which had now forced its way to the front of her mind.

'Did Mr. Bannister say anything about bringing his son with him? – Mr. Marc Bannister who, after all, *did* compose "The Exile".'

'I told you. He never mentioned "The Exile".' Madame Marburger spoke briskly. 'It may have nothing to do with that at all. A man like Quentin Bannister has many irons in the fire.'

'I know.' Gail still looked slightly troubled. 'But, you see, Mr. Bannister and his son don't always seem to see eye to eye about things. Frankly, I don't think Mr. Marc Bannister was much in my favour. I shouldn't like to think his father might be going behind his back.'

Madame Marburger looked astonished, as well she might.

'I think, my dear,' she said drily, 'that you're rather exaggerating your own importance. I hardly think the Bannisters would be quarrelling over a singing student, however gifted.'

'Of course, that's true.' Gail coloured suddenly. 'I don't know what made me think – imagine—'

'Nor do I, quite frankly,' cut in her teacher, in a tone which discouraged any further discussion. 'No doubt Mr. Bannister will get in touch with me about a convenient time to hear you when he is coming to town. All you have to do is see you are in good vocal shape when the time comes. You were not at your best today. There was a very poor degree of concentration.'

Gail accepted this rebuke humbly, feeling it was probably justified. For it had been difficult to concentrate on routine work when an exciting and faintly mysterious prospect was beckoning. But, try as she would to keep her teacher's trenchant words in mind, something deeper than logic made her speculate a trifle uneasily about Quentin Bannister's latest move.

She thought at first that she would tell Oliver about it. Then she decided that the less said about it the better. She was not at all a secretive girl, but she sensed instinctively that the Bannisters did not always let their right hand know what their left hand was doing. And if anyone presumed to pass on information to the wrong quarter, that person would be extremely unwise.

When she went out with Oliver that week-end, therefore, she made no mention of his father's approach to her teacher. And this was made all the easier by the fact that he was full of his own affairs.

'I want you to meet Tom Mallender,' he informed her. 'He's the chap who is collaborating with me over these revue sketches. I've told him about you, and that you know how to hold your tongue in the early stages and not talk about our work until we're ready to talk about it ourselves. I'm to take you along to his studio this evening, and we're going to try out one or two numbers on you. Is that O.K. with you?'

'I'll say it is!' Gail was immensely gratified, as well as curious. 'What do you want me to do? Just listen?'

'And express a reasonably intelligent opinion. We're getting so involved and enthusiastic ourselves that it's difficult to be self-critical. We need another opinion. But if we're as good as we sometimes think we are we can't risk taking most people into our confidence. They'd start blabbing about it, and then the whole thing would go off at half-cock.'

'I'll do my best,' Gail promised. 'And I'll be silent discretion itself outside the studio.'

After a hasty dinner – over which, to her surprise, Oliver seemed as nervous as a prima donna on a first night – he drove her to his friend's studio and presented her to Tom Mallender.

In contrast to Oliver, Tom was perfectly cool and collected.

'Oliver says you're a good, average judge,' he observed, as he poured her a long cool drink.

'I don't know that I am,' Gail protested. 'I'm very

happy to listen and give my views for what they're worth. But you're probably much better judges yourselves. If you can actually compose these things you must have a pretty good idea about standards.'

'Difficult when it's your own stuff.' Tom Mallender shook his head. 'There are times when I think we're turning out rot, and others when I wonder how the world managed so far without us.'

Gail laughed, but Oliver growled, 'Don't be an ass. It's pretty ordinary stuff, really. Only maybe it has a certain twist—'

'There you are! That's what I mean,' Tom said resignedly. 'When my spirits are up his are down, and vice versa. Play her something, Oliver, and stop glooming.'

So Oliver went to the piano, ran his hands over the keys for a moment or two, and then began to play an enchanting, half sad, half impudent little air. Without even bothering to get up from his chair where he was lounging, Tom began to sing, in a thin but appealing baritone. And the words he sang were, like the music, just on the perilous edge between pathos and self-mockery.

The whole thing was funny and sad, absurd and yet nostalgic. And the music so entirely echoed the words that the two seemed to have come from one brain.

'Why, boys, it's *adorable*!' cried Gail when they had finished. 'The kind of tune everyone will be singing within days! And it's so funny – and sad – and—' she sought for the right word and came up with it – 'so *stylish*. Almost everything today is so brash and coarse and amateurish. This has quality. Play something else, Oliver, play something else.'

They caught her mood of enthusiasm. And Oliver played and Tom sang, and presently Gail also came to the piano and, leaning over Oliver's shoulder to look at the roughly scribbled scraps of manuscript, she sang too.

Once she said, 'That's a bit trite. But perhaps it doesn't matter. It's quite a good tune.' And another time she said, 'That's heaven! You can afford to repeat it.'

At last Oliver turned and looked at her with new respect and said, 'How do you know so much about it?'

'I don't. It's just a sort of instinct. I'm the completely average girl with a little bit up here—' she tapped her head. 'This is what everyone reasonably intelligent is longing for. They're sick of bawling and crudities. They want spice without vulgarity, a touch of romance without too much sugar, nostalgia without self-pity. You know – *you just can't fail!*'

'Isn't she a honey?' said Oliver. 'What did I tell you?' And he got up and kissed her.

'You didn't tell me enough,' replied Tom, and he also kissed her. Then they opened a bottle of champagne and were wildly gay for half an hour. After which Tom said,

'You've got quite a nice voice yourself.'

'She's got a wonderful voice!' exclaimed Oliver indignantly. 'Why, my brother Marc is quite seriously considering her for the lead in his new opera.'

'You don't want to waste yourself on anything like that,' Tom told Gail, with shocking indifference to the higher values. 'Try her on the Spanish number, Oliver.'

'We haven't really decided how it should go,' Oliver objected.

'Let her decide,' replied Tom grandly. And they all crowded back to the piano, where Oliver played a pseudo-Spanish air with an over-exaggeration of rhythm which made it subtly funny.

'Here you are – here are the words.' Tom thrust a piece of paper into her hand, and they both watched her intently while she read them through.

Then she said, 'Play it without that extra emphasis, Oliver. Play it straight.'

'But it's not meant to be straight,' Oliver objected. 'It's a skit on all the skirt-twirling and castanet-clicking that one is so sick of.'

'I know. But play it straight,' she insisted. 'I'm going to sing it that way.'

He did as she ordered. And, in her 'dark velvet' voice, she sang the song with the utmost simplicity. Not a note was exaggerated, not a shade of pathos was overdone. There was even a sort of desperate dignity about it. And at the end they both turned again to look at her, and Tom said in an awed tone, 'She's right, you know.'

'But we're right too, in a way,' Oliver said.

'Of course you are! That's why it has to be done both ways,' declared Gail, on a sudden inspiration. 'What is the scene, anyway? How were you going to use it?'

'We hadn't really decided.' That was Tom. 'It was to have a conventional Spanish background, of course. A sort of overdone act put on for the tourists. It was to be played for laughs, with everyone recognizing the sort of thing they expect to get on holiday but which has nothing to do with the real Spain. I don't think, really, that it would bear the weight of a serious presentation, Gail.'

'Yes, it would.' She was thinking rapidly. 'The girl who sings it does overdo it at first. It's her big card for attracting the men. You can have what laughs you like in the way she makes fools of them. But then there's someone she really wants, and he just walks past without even noticing her. Or perhaps he looks at her with distaste. And when they've all gone and she's alone, she sings the song again. Exactly the same words and music. Only this time it means something that she's never even realized herself before. It *could* be a heart-stopper, done that way.'

'The girl's a genius!' Tom mopped his forehead with his handkerchief. 'We'd better take her into partnership. I'm nearly sure she's right. If we—'

Suddenly they were all three talking together and, with Oliver playing on the piano and Tom striking out words and substituting others on his battered piece of paper, they then and there worked out the song which was to capture all London in less than a year's time.

It was late when Oliver took her home, and they walked hand in hand through the cool autumn night, while the stars seemed to lean out of heaven. And inevitably he kissed her goodnight when he left her.

Dead tired now and feeling a certain reaction from the excitement of the evening, Gail slowly climbed the stairs to her small attic flat, wondering quite seriously if she were in love with Oliver.

The next morning, in retrospect, the whole evening seemed a little mad and quite incredible. Had those numbers really been as brilliant and witty as they had seemed at the time? Was her suggestion about the Spanish item a stroke of genius or a rather silly gimmick?

As she ran through the rain to the church where she was to sing that morning, she asked herself these questions and found no answer. And as she sang her way with genuine feeling through one of the noblest of Bach's airs, she felt faintly guilty about her performance the night before. It all seemed rather a long way from Bach! and she doubted if Madame Marburger would have approved.

But later, at home, while she washed her 'smalls' and sewed on a couple of buttons and wrote a long letter home, she paused from time to time to hum the Spanish air. And she knew instinctively that this was something people would love and remember, and associate always with some special occasion in their own lives.

For several days she heard nothing from Oliver. Then he telephoned and told her that he and Tom were so busy recasting some of their work and adding to it that he had no time for anything else.

'You don't mind, do you?' he asked rather absently.

'Not at all. I'm glad to know that inspiration is flowing so freely,' she replied with a laugh.

'It isn't, really. Sometimes we're terribly stuck, and then we quarrel like hell,' Oliver admitted. 'Then we remember how thrilled you were, and we decide it's worthwhile going on. What are you doing?'

'The usual.' She was touched and pleased to have been of some use to the gifted couple. 'Working hard and chasing the odd engagement. I'm off to a lesson now.'

'Then go along, bless you. I won't keep you.' And he rang off so abruptly that Gail felt she was definitely of secondary interest at the moment. She didn't hold it against him. She was sufficiently dedicated herself to understand that there were times when the dearest and most interesting person counted as nothing beside the pursuit of an artistic ideal.

When she arrived at Madame Marburger's studio she became aware that her teacher was speaking to someone, and she hesitated outside the door, wondering if the previous pupil's lesson had not quite ended. Then a deep, attractive, authoritative voice cut in and, suddenly recognizing it with an upsurge of excitement, Gail tapped on the door and went in.

Quentin Bannister was walking up and down, talking animatedly, while Elsa Marburger sat there listening to him with an odd mixture of amusement and respect.

'Here she is!' Quentin Bannister turned to Gail and took her hand. 'We were talking about you, and I'm trying to persuade Madame Marburger that your talents lie much more in the direction of the theatre than the concert and oratorio platform.'

'I am not entirely convinced.' Madame Marburger smiled a little distantly. 'But I see no reason why Gail shouldn't avail herself of the opportunity you offer, and make an experimental digression into opera at this point. Will you explain to her?'

Quentin Bannister made a slightly impatient movement of his expressive hand, a little as though he deplored having to explain himself once he had made up his mind.

'Gail already knows most of the situation,' he said. But he turned to her then. 'There is a strong probability of "The Exile" being put on in London in the near future,' he explained. 'And, in my view, you should be seriously considered for the part of Anya. As you know, Marc and I are not entirely at one on this. But he sees you only as you are now. Being much more experienced, I can see you as you would be after careful coaching. By the time we come to the real auditions I want you to be thoroughly prepared. Indeed—' he smiled with a satisfied air – 'I want you to be several jumps ahead of anyone else who applies and comes to it "cold" as it were.'

'But is that quite fair?' protested Gail.

'*Fair?*' Quentin Bannister repeated the word as though he found it entirely unacceptable. 'What do you mean by *fair*? This isn't some silly competition, with rules and regulations. It's a professional audition, and you need to present yourself in the best light, which you certainly couldn't do as you are now.'

'Yes – I see,' said Gail meekly.

'Then don't make stupid interruptions,' he told her sharply. 'I have brought you a copy of the score. There are only three or four of them as yet, so take care of it. I want you to learn the part, and I have arranged with your teacher that each one of your Tuesday lessons shall be on this work alone. I come to London on Tuesdays and shall be present at your lessons. And if I can't convey to you more of this role than anyone else in London, I'm not the man I think I am.'

It was so patently – and engagingly – obvious that he thought himself capable of anything that both Gail and Elsa Marburger smiled at him and took him entirely at his own valuation.

'Well—' he held out both his hands to Elsa Marburger in a warm and expansive gesture – 'I congratulate you, my dear, on the work you have done with this gifted child, and I rely on you to co-operate over this.'

Then he turned to Gail.

'As for you, Gail, I promise nothing, of course, and you must not be disappointed if in the end the prize is not yours. The experience will be invaluable in any case.'

'I know that. And I'm grateful.' She put her hand into his.

'Just one thing more.' His hand tightened on hers as she was about to withdraw it. 'This is a completely private matter between you and me and your admirable teacher. In a sense, I suppose you could say I am stealing a march on Marc. I prefer to put it that I am backing my own more experienced judgment against his, for his own ultimate good. I want him to hear you as you really *can be* before he makes the final judgment about the casting of his work. Is that understood?'

'Oh, yes,' said Gail. And then, quite irrepressibly, she added, 'You're quite sure that you do know better than

Marc about this?'

'Why, of course,' said Quentin Bannister simply. 'And that's why this small subterfuge is justified, and why I must ask you to say nothing whatever to Marc about it.'

'I'm not likely to see him anyway,' Gail observed practically.

'That's true. He completely underestimated you.'

Then he bade them both a courteous good-bye, and went on his triumphant way.

'It must,' said Elsa Marburger at last, 'be very difficult to live with a genius.'

'I was just thinking the same thing,' replied Gail, and they both laughed. But then they became entirely serious and turned to examine the score of 'The Exile' together.

The original lesson lengthened into twice its usual extent and finally Madame Marburger said, 'Go home now and put in some hard work on that first scene. What are you doing over the week-end?'

Gail had been hoping that Oliver and Tom Mallender were intending to see her at the week-end. But work – and the great opportunity – had to come first. So there was no more than a second's pause before she said, 'I'm more or less free.'

'Then you had better come and see me on Saturday afternoon. By the time Mr. Bannister comes on Tuesday, you and I shall need to be pretty familiar with the early part of this work at least.'

With hardly a pang, Gail jettisoned the possibility of an inspiring afternoon with Oliver and Tom. Instead, she thanked her teacher for her willingness to give up *her* Saturday and, having carefully put away the precious score in her music case, she said good-bye and went out into the afternoon sunshine.

In her present state of excitement it was impossible to sit quietly on a bus. So she walked instead – from Regents Park down to Oxford Street. And all the way she was turning over in her mind the amazing thing which had happened to her – and the implications of Quentin Bannister's arbitrary arrangement.

That she was incredibly lucky to have him take this interest in her was beyond question. If his judgment were right – and who was she to question the judgment of Quentin Bannister? – she would stand a very good chance of getting the role of Anya when the time came. What that could mean to her future career was something so dazzling that even the afternoon sunshine seemed to pale before such a prospect.

She crossed Oxford Street and, hardly noticing where she was going, continued on down Bond Street. As she did so, she was aware that somewhere there was a cloud on the general radiance of Mr. Bannister's plan. It was nothing to do with lack of confidence in his judgment, nor even a diffidence about her own gifts, for she was determined to work on this role as she had never worked before. What troubled her – and she faced the fact now – was the idea that all this was to be done without the slightest reference to the man most concerned.

It was, as she had protested to Oliver, *Marc's* opera. Surely he was entitled to know about every step taken towards its successful presentation?

She sighed unhappily, for she had accepted Quentin Bannister's offer on his terms. What else could she do? If he liked to go his own autocratic way, and keep Marc in the dark about what he was doing, it was not for her to interfere in family politics. But it occurred to her suddenly that she was being asked to keep altogether too many family secrets for the Bannisters. First Oliver had sworn her to secrecy over his work with Tom Mallender. And now Quentin Bannister high-handedly demanded that she should preserve unreasonable secrecy over his meddling in Marc's affairs.

'Meddling' was not the most gracious – or grateful – way of describing the magnificent offer which had been made to her. And, feeling both guilty and bewildered, Gail paused to look into a shop window. Not that she really examined the beautiful china displayed there with any special interest. She had merely come to a standstill in an effort to sort out her own confused thoughts.

And then a voice behind her said, 'Well, what do you like best in that window?' and she swung round sharply to find Marc Bannister at her elbow, a slight smile of amused inquiry on his face.

'I – I don't know,' she stammered, overwhelmed by the absurd idea that she had pretty well conjured him up out of her own thoughts.

'Then look again,' he said, and confusedly she brought her attention to bear on the display in the window.

'Th-that one, I think.' She swallowed nervously and indicated a smug, fat eighteenth-century Cupid who was smiling as he placed an arrow to his bow.

'He is rather nice, isn't he?' Marc bent to examine him. 'Come on in and I'll buy him for you.'

'But I couldn't let you!' she protested. 'He's probably frightfully expensive. And anyway—'

'I'd like to. And I owe you something for half spoiling your week-end visit.'

'You don't! I loved every minute of it.'

'Oh, not every minute,' he reminded her.

And, before she knew quite what he was doing, he had swept her into the shop, had the Cupid taken from the window, and was handing over an embarrassing number of notes for the smug little creature.

'You can't,' she whispered agitatedly, even as the figure was being shrouded in tissue paper and placed in an ornamental box.

'But I have,' he pointed out. And presently the box was placed in her hand and they were outside in Bond Street once more, and she was trying incoherently to thank him.

'It's nothing – if you really like it. Come and have tea with me,' Marc said. 'We're almost at the Ritz and they do a good tea there.'

She could hardly refuse, considering he had just bought her such a charming gift. Anyway, she discovered suddenly, she didn't want to refuse. On the contrary, she was curiously elated by the prospect of tea with Marc Bannister on her own.

'Give me your case.' He held out his hand for her music case, and she surrendered it helplessly, wondering as she did so what he would have said if he could have known that it contained one of the few copies of his own operatic score.

CHAPTER FOUR

By the time they entered the lounge at the Ritz Gail had recovered herself a little, although she still felt a nervous tremor every time she thought what her music case contained. Then, as they sat down at a table, she glanced down at the parcel she was carrying and exclaimed,

'I haven't really thanked you properly for this beautiful present! I'm afraid I was too stunned and surprised to find the right words. But I'm simply enchanted with it — and longing to have another look at it.'

'Then unwrap it and look.' He smiled across at her with a faint touch of indulgence.

'It's so beautifully done up—' she began. Then pleasurable curiosity got the better of her and she carefully opened the box, undid the wrappings and stood her china Cupid on the tea-table.

All the time Marc Bannister watched her, with amusement, but a certain air of pleasure too.

'I've never owned anything so lovely before,' she said earnestly.

'Oh, nonsense! you must have.' His was the amused surprise of a man who seldom had to ask the price before buying something he wanted.

'But it's true.' She looked up and laughed. 'I like my flat, but it's furnished with the oddest bits and pieces, and most of my domestic china came from Woolworths. I have got a nice little Bavarian vase that a friend on holiday brought me. But it's not in this class at all. Is this French?'

'No. Meissen, I expect.' He took it in his strong, well-

74

shaped hands and turned it over, to show her the crossed swords on the base of the figure. 'It's quite a good period,' he added, examining it more closely. 'I'm glad you like it.'

'I love it,' she said shyly. 'There really wasn't the slightest reason why you should give me a present – but I love it.'

'I told you – I owed you something for spoiling your week-end.'

'But you didn't, you know. There were only a few annoying moments. Anyway, you were unhappy and had to take it out on someone, didn't you?' she added without rancour.

'That sounds a pretty petty explanation,' he said, with a slight grimace. 'How did you know I was unhappy? – if I was.'

The tea was brought just then, and she poured out while she considered her reply.

'Usually when people are unreasonably bad-tempered they are either frightened or miserable,' she observed at last. 'I can't quite imagine your being frightened, so I suppose you were miserable.'

He was silent at that and after a moment she asked candidly, 'Were you very much in love with Lena Dorman?'

'Very much. Though I don't know why I should tell *you* about it,' he added rather stiffly.

'No reason at all,' Gail agreed cheerfully, as she bit into a delectable sandwich. 'What else shall we talk about?'

He laughed at that, and then said, rather as though he couldn't help it, 'She was in love with me too at first.'

'Oh?' Gail could not quite keep the note of scepticism out of her voice, and he added reluctantly, 'In her way, I mean.'

75

'I'm bound to say I think it would always be a very self-seeking way,' Gail told him kindly. 'But no doubt you know that for yourself. Still, one doesn't stop loving people just because one recognizes their faults. If you still feel so badly about Lena, why don't you put a line under the shabby way she treated you, and start again? Forgive her – or whatever you like to call it.'

He stirred his tea moodily and said without looking up, 'You know the answer to that, don't you?'

'There are two or three possible answers,' replied Gail. 'I don't know which one you give yourself. It could be that you feel you could never trust her again. It could be that your pride means more to you than your affections. Or it could be just that you know perfectly well she's had enough of you anyway.'

'It's the last one,' he said, and then they were both silent.

'I'm so sorry.' Gail spoke at last. 'I'm afraid there's not much help for that, is there? And I won't tell you that you're well rid of her, because you probably know that too. One does get over most things, though – if that's any consolation. Try going out with some other girl instead, even if—'

'You, for instance,' he interrupted sardonically.

'Oh, I wasn't thinking of me,' she assured him coolly. 'I don't think I'm your type at all. But lots of girls would be very happy to be noticed by you. You're good-looking, quite well heeled, on the way to being famous, and attractive in your way.'

'Why don't you think you're my type?' was what he said in reply to all that.

'Well, your week-end reactions certainly didn't suggest I was, did they? Anyway, I imagine you like your womenfolk to be rather sophisticated, and I'm not a bit that.'

'No, you're not, are you?' he agreed, with rather unflattering emphasis. But then he added unexpectedly, 'I think that's why I like you.'

'Oh—' she looked down at the Cupid again, a trifle put out by this plain statement.

'Come out with me this evening, Gail,' he exclaimed suddenly. 'I have tickets for the Verdi Requiem at the Festival Hall. Oscar Warrender is conducting and Anthea is singing the soprano part.'

'I—' she hesitated, longing to go, yet frightened still at the thought of the score in her music case. In addition, she had a vague sense of disloyalty in accepting Marc's invitation while sharing his father's subterfuge – however well that might be meant. 'I'm not dressed for anything like that,' she said at last, glancing down at her very ordinary everyday attire.

'You look all right to me,' he replied. 'But if you want to dress up, I imagine you have plenty of time to go home first. It doesn't start until eight. Where do you live?'

'Just off Hampstead Heath.'

'Well, then—' he glanced at his watch. 'Meet me near the box office at the Hall at twenty minutes to eight. And,' he added with a sudden smile, 'I'll take you round afterwards to meet the Warrenders, if you like.'

'You *will*?' Her eyes shone with excitement. 'Do you know them quite well?'

'Yes, of course.' She rather gathered that he knew everyone in the musical world quite well. 'Warrender is interested to some degree in "The Exile", as a matter of fact.'

She trembled again at the mention of that dangerous title. But the invitation was altogether too enticing for her to refuse.

77

'I'll come, of course. And thank you a thousand times!'

'The pleasure is equally mine,' he told her with that half mocking, wholly charming smile of his. 'Can I get you a taxi?' as they rose to go.

'Oh, no, thank you. I'll go by Tube.' She carefully picked up her re-wrapped parcel.

'Don't forget your music case.' He picked that up. 'What are you working on at the moment?'

'Several things,' she exclaimed in great confusion, and she more or less snatched the case from his hand, lest he should look inside. 'I'll have to hurry now, if I'm to get home and back. Thank you for my lovely tea – and my wonderful present – and for the invitation to the concert. Thank you for *everything*, in fact.'

'And thank *you* for being so appreciative,' he said with a smile as he parted from her outside the Ritz.

As Gail ran down the steps to the Tube station she was aware of a flutter of excitement and anxiety and rapture and confusion such as she had never known before. She told herself it was the mixture of uneasiness because of the secrecy which Quentin Bannister had forced upon her and the sheer delight of being taken to what would un-doubtedly be one of the great performances of the season.

'I'm terribly lucky!' she thought, feeling sorry for all the other people in the Tube train who were not going to the concert and didn't know Marc Bannister.

And didn't know Marc Bannister.

Suddenly the realization hit her, almost like a physical blow, that what irradiated this whole experience was the fact that Marc was taking her, Marc had bought her that lovely present, Marc had said he liked her.

'Well, why not?' she asked herself defiantly. Hadn't she herself enumerated to him the reasons why a girl might very well like to be taken out by him? She had been trying to cheer him for the loss of Lena, of course. She certainly had not had herself in mind when she uttered those words. But now she saw, with sobering clarity, that what she had really been putting into words was how he appeared to *her*.

She arrived at the end of her journey before she had fully examined what the implications of that discovery might be. Which was just as well, she told herself. Otherwise she might have got the impression that it was all rather more important than it really was.

After that she was too busy hurrying to her flat, changing, snatching a cup of coffee and a sandwich, and setting off for town again, for her to have time for foolish introspection.

She was in good time at the Festival Hall, but he was already there waiting for her, looking extremely distinguished in his dinner jacket.

'Goodness! You didn't go back to Sussex and change, did you?' she greeted him rather perkily.

'No.' He smiled down at her. 'I have a flat of my own in town.'

'Oh, I see. You look terribly distinguished and exactly as though you might be the composer of an important opera,' Gail told him.

'Thank you for those heartening words. You yourself look enchanting,' he replied. 'What do you call that particular shade of green?'

'I don't know,' Gail confessed. 'But it's pretty, isn't it?'

'No,' he said. 'It's lovely. And so are you.'

'Well—' Gail suddenly found she had come to the end of her stock of banter, so she looked round instead, and was more than ever glad that she had rushed home to change. For it was, largely speaking, a well-dressed audience, sufficiently well-bred to know that a festive occasion requires a little effort from the audience as well as the artists.

She was too sensible a person to demand this particular atmosphere for every occasion, of course. Music-making was, she knew, deeper than any externals, and could be appreciated in much humbler circumstances than these. But there was no denying the fact that the hall looked splendid, that a subtle air of festivity permeated the place, and that as the famous conductor came on, and the orchestra and choir rose to their feet, one felt an upsurge of something very much more than good, solid pleasure.

Then the four soloists filed on to the platform, and Gail looked at Anthea Warrender and thought how beautiful and distinguished she looked. And she remembered the romantic story of how *she* had been a mere singing student once and Warrender had picked her out, trained her, bullied her, coaxed her to stardom and finally married her. It was a good story, and Gail found herself hoping that at least some of the romantic details were true.

She doubted if anyone – by which she meant herself – could *really* fall in love with someone as arrogant and unapproachable as Oscar Warrender. But once the performance had started she fell completely under his spell, realizing that there was something in that strange mixture of ruthlessness and tenderness which not only drew the last ounce of artistic effort from his players and singers but perhaps belonged also to the man himself.

After a while, in company with most of the audience, she began to feel that she too was part of the performance. And then it became not a performance but an experience, and she was aware of that strange, glorious feeling of being in some way transported.

This is, of course, the special gift of the genius, as opposed to the excellent, worthy artist. To transport us from the mundane world of everyday to some other dimension of thought and experience, so that we too are better, happier, greater than we thought ourselves to be. It is something one can neither teach nor learn, but to those who have it the world instinctively pays ungrudging tribute. (With the melancholy exception of those who are too small-minded to love greatness anyway.)

As the last notes of the 'Libera me' floated away into what seemed like eternity a deathly hush fell on the hall. Then the applause broke forth in a perfect storm. Gail found herself on her feet, cheering with the rest, and once she turned an excited face upon Marc Bannister and exclaimed, 'Oh, you darling for bringing me! It was wonderful – wonderful. I've never heard it sound like that before. I wouldn't have missed it for the world!'

'Nor would I,' he said, and he smiled down into her radiant face, before they both turned once more to the platform to applaud the returning soloists.

Finally the audience insisted on Warrender taking a solo bow. But as the applause broke out afresh, he simply took the score in his hand and held it up, so that the one name 'Verdi' was plain for all to see.

'Oh, that's lovely!' exclaimed Gail, greatly moved. 'He can't really be arrogant, after all.'

'As a man he is rather,' Marc assured her with a slight laugh. 'As a musician not at all. Come along, and we'll see if we can fight our way round backstage.'

It was something of a struggle, literally, to make their way through the enthusiastic crowds. But presently one of the ushers recognized Marc and made way for him and his companion.

'Good evening, sir. Mr. Quentin Bannister not here this evening?'

'No. He had to go back to the country,' Marc said.

'A pity! *He* would have known how to appreciate to-night.'

'Indeed, yes,' replied Marc courteously. But Gail noticed a slight tightening of his mouth, and she wondered if this were the sort of thing Oliver had meant when he said it was difficult being merely the son of one's father, instead of someone in one's own right.

As they reached the door of the conductor's room, someone exclaimed, 'Hello, Marc! Are you just going in to see Oscar? Come with me.' And Gail realized that it was Anthea Warrender who had caught her companion lightly by the arm.

Marc performed rapid introductions, the famous young soprano smiled warmly at Gail and then said in a low voice, 'The opera is terrific, Marc. Makes me almost wish I were a contralto!'

'You like it?' Marc flushed, a rare sign of pleasure with him. 'I didn't know you'd even seen the score.'

'But of course! I went right through it with Oscar. But come and hear what he has to say about it.' And she gently but very firmly put aside the remaining people in their path and led the way into the conductor's room.

In spite of the strenuous evening behind him, Oscar Warrender was standing in animated conversation with a man who looked vaguely familiar to Gail. And as Anthea said, 'Oh, Max—' she realized that it was the producer, Max Egon.

Immediately the conversation was flowing round and about her, and she saw, with a degree of pleasure which surprised her, that they were all speaking to Marc in a congratulatory way. Not just the uninformed congratulation of the politely enthusiastic, but the completely knowledgeable assessment of those who were saluting an equal in their own chosen world.

No one thought to introduce her further, and she didn't mind. She stood slightly to one side, happy that Marc should be acclaimed in his own right, questioned and praised by people he knew and valued. She had never seen him look quite like that – brilliant and happy, tremendously lively, and virtually the centre of the group.

'Join us for supper,' Warrender said finally. 'Max is coming with us. And the four of us can discuss all this over—'

'There are five of us,' Anthea put in kindly. 'Miss Rostall is with Marc.'

The conductor's glance took in Miss Rostall for the first time – without much pleasure. And Gail rose to the occasion with admirable self-sacrifice.

'It's very kind of you, but I'm afraid I simply have to go,' she explained, with a convincing air of regretful firmness. 'Marc was good enough to bring me round to add my congratulations to everyone else's. I just want to thank you for an unforgettable evening. But now I have a train to catch.'

Warrender accepted this immediately, with a courteous but unmistakable gesture of dismissal. Marc started forward, however,

'No – I can find my way out,' Gail assured him. But he insisted on coming with her as far as the exit.

'You could have joined us,' he told her. 'Warrender wouldn't really have minded.'

'He certainly *would*!' Gail retorted with a laugh. 'And I don't blame him. He wants a thoroughly professional discussion with you. To have a casual girl-friend of the evening included would have inhibited things dreadfully.'

'Warrender is not capable of being inhibited where his work is concerned,' Marc said with a smile. 'But thank you for being so understanding. More than Lena would have been in like circumstances,' he added with a flash of wry humour. 'Come out with me another time, Gail.'

'I'd like to.' She spoke without a moment's hesitation. And then, to her astonishment, Marc Bannister bent his head and lightly kissed her cheek.

'You gave me good advice this afternoon,' he said before he turned to go back into the hall. 'I shall bear it in mind.'

And Gail, as she went on her way to the station, had to resist a distinct impulse to put up her hand against the cheek he had kissed. It had been the lightest of salutes. A good deal less significant, she supposed, than the kiss his brother had bestowed upon her after the exciting evening with Tom Mallender. But it had a value all its own.

Only the faintest disappointment lingered as she thought of the others going out to supper together, to discuss 'The Exile'. But for her certainty that she would have been a slight brake on the wheel of Marc's interests, she would have loved to have gone too. Anthea's quick kindness would have made it possible. Marc's willingness to include her confirmed that. And possibly within half an hour Warrender himself would have accepted her into the magic circle. (After all, she *had* been tried out in the leading role!) But she knew instinctively that Marc's friendly impulse to take her to the concert was on an entirely different level from the importance of talking about his work with Oscar Warrender.

'Don't over-estimate your importance, my girl,' she told herself, as she walked up the hill to her flat. And when she let herself in, and saw the smug little Cupid sitting on the mantelpiece, playing with his bow and arrows, she went over and addressed him.

'I could have gone out to supper with him,' she said, 'and I didn't. It wasn't only tact. I wanted the best for him. I like him – in spite of a bad beginning. And you, you fat little wretch, are partly responsible!'

But the Cupid just smiled and went on fitting an arrow to his bow. He didn't need anyone to tell him what *his* work was.

The following morning Oliver telephoned early to say that Tom and he wanted her to come over to the studio and spend Saturday afternoon with them.

'Things are going well. And we want you in on them,' he explained flatteringly.

'Oh, Oliver, I'm terribly sorry! I can't. I have an extra lesson with Madame Marburger,' Gail said.

'But you won't be doing that all the afternoon, for goodness' sake!'

'I might be. I don't know how long the lesson might last.'

'Why? What are you working on that requires all that special grind?' he wanted to know, the note of irritation in his voice betraying impatience with anything that threatened to slow down his own plans.

'There's the possibility of an important audition coming up and I want—'

'What audition?'

'Oh, I can't explain now. Madame Marburger has offered to give up *her* Saturday afternoon. I can hardly quibble about mine, can I? Couldn't I come along to the studio later? – in the early evening?'

'I suppose you could,' he agreed rather ungraciously. 'Get away as soon as you can. Why can't you tell me what it's all about? What's the mystery?'

'There's no mystery,' Gail said, her heart thumping rather heavily at the realization that she was handling this badly. She should never have used the word 'audition'. It led too easily to the very subject she was not to discuss. 'I'll tell you more about it when I see you,' she promised hastily, and then she rang off.

She would manage to think of something before she had to face him in person. Meanwhile, she gave all her thoughts and energy to working on that first scene.

Gail was a quick learner and found little difficulty in the actual memorizing. What was much more important and difficult was the phrasing, the right emphasis, the conveying of a mood by the inflection of the voice. The actual structure of the music was deceptively simple, but she realized that it required a very subtle variation of tone colour, and after the first hour or two she was completely fascinated by the work.

When she went to her lesson on Saturday afternoon she was already beginning to live the part, and every minute of that long afternoon was a joy to her.

Even when the lesson was over and she was on her way to Tom Mallender's studio she had some difficulty in switching her thoughts from 'The Exile' to the affairs of Oliver and his friend. But both the young men greeted her with such genuine pleasure that she felt her heart warm to them.

To her relief, Oliver forgot to ask about the audition she had mentioned. Indeed he made no enquiries at all until she said something about being a little tired and being glad to relax. At that point Oliver observed,

'You're working too hard. All that oratorio stuff takes it out of you. What was the big date, by the way? Are the Royal Choral waiting to snatch you up?'

'Hardly!' Gail laughed. And even as she was wondering

how she should change the subject, Tom exclaimed,

'Forget about all that and come in with us, Gail.'

'What do you mean?' She looked startled.

'We're heading for the top in our own line of business. We're convinced of that. And we'd like you to be with us. Oliver will enjoy writing things specially for you, won't you, Noll?'

'More than I can say,' Oliver smiled at her. 'But I didn't dare to bring up the subject.'

'You can't be serious?' Gail glanced quickly from one to the other of them.

'We're completely serious,' Tom assured her. 'You've got something, Gail. And it's something that belongs to *our* line. You don't want to spend your life drudging away at the odd oratorio engagement, or small operatic bits and pieces—'

She started to speak, but he said, 'No, let me finish. You haven't got the kind of equipment that makes a prima donna, and the second and third line stuff in that world is pretty thankless. There are dozens – hundreds – of good, capable singers who are never going to scratch much more than a crust. And unless you're damn lucky you're likely to be one of them. Whereas, if you throw in your lot with us, we'll make you a star.'

'I couldn't even think of it!' Gail was quite white with mingled anger and dismay. 'You don't really know anything about my particular gifts, such as they are. I don't presume to see myself as a world-shaking prima donna, it's true. But I think I have it in me to get pretty near the top of the tree. I'm not only speaking from my own hopes and beliefs. My teacher thinks very well of me, and I've had quite a lot of encouragement from—' She stopped, for she had almost stumbled on to the forbidden topic.

Instead, she turned rather angrily on Oliver and exclaimed, 'Do *you* think the same as Tom? You've heard me in the more serious stuff, and you've had some experience. Do *you* honestly think I'll never make my way in the world of serious music?'

'No, I don't think that.' Oliver looked faintly uncomfortable. 'I think that with luck you might indeed, as you say, get somewhere near the top of the tree – in this country at least. Even without luck you'd probably make a reasonable living. You're a good oratorio singer, and there's always a demand for that. But it's a heartbreaking life if one *doesn't* have the luck, Gail. It's no good saying anything else. I've seen a good deal of that, one way and another.'

'And what about the luck that's required for *your* kind of musical life?' she retorted. 'Are you going to tell me that luck isn't desperately needed there too?'

'Of course it is. But—' Oliver looked at Tom and Tom nodded as though to confirm whatever Oliver was going to say.

'Gail, we both think this *is* our luck,' Oliver said earnestly. 'Yours and ours. We think that together we could be a terrific combination. The spark we struck the other evening isn't just a passing thing. It was the kind of spark that lights a bonfire. Luck doesn't always come in the same guise. Our luck is that we have all come together at the right moment. You inspire us and we inspire you. We belong together as a team. Tom and I are both convinced of that. *That* is our luck. That we found each other.'

'But I couldn't, Oliver dear!' All the anger had gone out of her now, but she simply could not let herself follow his line of reasoning. 'All my work and study – everything that I love and believe – belongs to what one calls serious music. Oh, don't think I'm underestimating what you two are doing. On the contrary, I think it's brilliant and I think it's going to succeed. Only it's not for me.'

'It is, you know,' said Tom, while Oliver remained silent. 'You've got just the right mixture of sentiment without sugariness and wit without cynicism. And you have style – quality. And the fact that you bring a really stunning voice to it all helps to lift the thing to a level far above the usual run of popular stuff.'

'But suppose you're wrong, Tom?' She faced him, not aggressively but realistically. 'You're gambling on your beliefs just as I suppose you might say I'm gambling on mine. I hate to say it, but, although we all think well of your big effort, it might *not* be a success – and my big effort might. It's a toss-up. You can't expect me to abandon the work of years on the strength of your belief in your own judgment, can you?'

'But what big effort in your own line have you got to put up against *our* proposition?' Tom asked bluntly. 'You say yourself that you have some minor engagements here and there—' He stopped as an odd expression came over her face. 'Well, what *have* you got?' he asked curiously.

And Oliver echoed, 'Yes, what have you got, Gail? Is this the big mystery?'

'N–no—' she began. But she could see his quick mind working, and she was not really surprised when he exclaimed,

'Is it something to do with "The Exile"?'

She was silent, not knowing at all how to handle the discussion now that it had taken this turn, and Oliver said earnestly, 'Gail dear, don't attach any importance to what Marc and my father said. They're quite capable of raising all sorts of hopes and then—'

'It's not that!' she interrupted desperately. 'It's not only what was said during that week-end. It's – oh, I suppose I just have to tell you. But please, please understand this is entirely between ourselves, and Marc certainly mustn't know, at *any* price. Your father genuinely wants me in the part of Anya, Oliver. He came to see Madame Marburger about it, and he's prepared to coach me himself, so that I shall show up at my very best when it comes to the real auditions. He thinks Marc is prejudiced and he's determined—'

'The old devil!' interjected Oliver rather admiringly. 'So he's determined to make Marc swallow you somehow.'

'I wouldn't put it like that.' Indeed Gail winced at the expression. 'He says – I suppose correctly – that he has had much more experience than Marc in knowing how an artist can sound after the proper coaching and guidance. He doesn't want Marc just to judge on that rather raw performance the other day. He's kind enough to say that he himself can assess the actual potential in me and that—'

'My father isn't "kind enough" for anything,' Oliver interrupted. 'He isn't what you mean by a kind man at all. If he says he can judge your real potential, it has nothing to do with kindness. He means just exactly what he says, and he's backing his fancy because he truly believes he can make the Anya of all Anyas out of you. The fact that Marc – the mere composer of the work – might think otherwise is not even interesting to him.'

Again Gail was silent, with something like dismay. And Oliver turned to his friend with a resigned shrug.

'I don't think we can offer anything to outweigh this, Tom. I'm sorry. I still think we could have been a grand team together. But we're not even in the business yet. And I agree with Gail – she can't afford to pass up my father's offer.'

Tom muttered something, but Gail looked gratefully at

Oliver.

'You won't breathe a word about all this outside this room, will you?' she said anxiously. 'I'll keep quiet about your work, and you must please keep quiet about mine. I don't really like being in this equivocal position, but those were your father's terms. And, as he said himself, it's really in Marc's best interests too, because if—'

'That's Father's story, and he's sticking to it?' suggested Oliver with a grin.

'Well, it is *true*, isn't it?'

'If Father turns out to be right – yes.' Oliver laughed. 'But I wouldn't much like the job of explaining that to Marc.'

'No one is going to have to explain it to Marc,' Gail protested, in some agitation. 'Least of all myself. If, when the time comes, he thinks I'm no good – well, I've had my chance and that's that. But if he thinks I'm really what he wants for his opera, he won't mind much about how I came to that point.'

'I hope he thinks you're no good,' observed Tom calmly.

'Tom, you beast!'

'Not at all. Like all geniuses, I'm entirely self-centred,' said Tom complacently. 'Why should I hope you succeed in something that will run counter to my own interests? Would you like to hear our latest number?'

'Yes, please.' Gail laughed crossly – but she laughed.

She came eagerly to the piano then, and suddenly the mood of optimism and inspiration was on them all again, and the evening was entirely gay and delightful after that.

On the way home, Oliver asked her one or two further questions about his father's project. Then he said, 'He'll have to hurry, Gail. And so will you. I understand Oscar

Warrender is interested in the work – even to the extent of possibly conducting it himself. That could mean some pretty early auditioning. He usually goes to the States towards the end of the year, and he would probably want to get most of the casting done before he went.'

'When did you hear that?' Gail asked quickly.

'Only this morning. I ran into Marc and he was rather full of the fact that he had supper with the Warrenders the other evening—'

'Yes, I know,' said Gail without thinking.

'You know?' Oliver looked at her in astonishment. 'How do you know?'

'Well—' she saw no reason why she should be secretive about *that* – 'we went to the Verdi Requiem together. And – and so I knew that he went out afterwards with the Warrenders and Max Egon.'

'You and *Marc* went to the Requiem together?' He stared at her and she nodded a trifle self-consciously.

'Look here, you funny girl, whose side are you on?' demanded Oliver.

'What do you mean? – whose side am I on?'

'Well, on the one hand you're backing up Father in his happy little ploys against Marc. And on the other you're running around to concerts with Marc himself. If that's not running with the hare and hunting with the hounds, I don't know what is. Mind your step, Gail, mind your step!' There was a genuine note of warning in his laugh. 'They're both of them quite dangerous men in their way, and you're rather too much of an innocent to be able to hold the balance between them.'

CHAPTER FIVE

In bed that night Gail thought long and earnestly about the way in which she had become involved with the Bannister family.

She was not prepared to accept Oliver's contention that Marc and his father were almost totally opposed to each other on most things. Out of sympathy with each other, perhaps. And each with a degree of arrogance and obstinacy which meant frequent clashes. But they were not, she felt sure, unmindful of each other's real qualities.

Oliver persisted in speaking as though his father's plan of coaching Gail secretly for the role of Anya constituted a definite move against Marc.

'But it could be in Marc's best interests,' she had protested. 'Your father probably does know better than Marc just how different an artist can seem and sound after some good coaching. You're willing to concede that, I suppose?'

'Yes, of course. In fact, there's almost nothing Father doesn't know about developing an artist's hidden potential,' Oliver agreed.

'Well then — that's it! Rather than argue it out with Marc, he prefers to prove his point by producing the finished article — me, in fact — at the right time. What's wrong with that?'

'Only the cool assumption that he knows better than Marc himself how Marc's character should be portrayed. There are half a dozen ways of presenting any character of importance. You know that as well as I do, Gail. I don't doubt that Father will perfect you as *he* sees Anya. But I question whether that will be exactly the way Marc – who created the girl – will necessarily see her.'

'Then he can say so, at the auditions. And that will be an end of it,' Gail countered.

'No.' Oliver shook his head slightly. 'He won't be the deciding factor at the auditions.'

'But it's his work!'

'I've told you before – the people responsible for getting this work on a stage, the people who will be taking the risks in fact, will have just as much say as the composer himself. Marc's will be one voice only at the discussions. Father will come up with his candidate, trained and coached to such a degree that she will inevitably seem streets ahead of the others in most respects. However instinctively Marc may feel that isn't his Anya, he won't have much chance of impressing the others with his ideas.'

'Oliver,' she said in a troubled voice, 'are you *against* my having the part of Anya? I thought you were—'

'No, dear! No, I'm not. I'm against Father's way of pulling the strings beforehand so that his word will carry more weight than Marc's, over something which is *Marc's* achievement.'

'Then you think I ought to give up now? tell your father I'm not willing to do things this way?'

'Good lord, no!' For a moment Oliver looked startled at having his arguments carried to what Gail regarded as their logical conclusion. 'I'm merely telling you to look at Father's actions in their real light. It may end, of course, with Marc also finding you his ideal Anya. In which case everyone will be happy. Except maybe Tom,' he added with a grin.

'You still trouble me,' Gail said slowly, though she smiled slightly over his last words. 'I find it difficult even to imagine a situation like this in any family. In my own, for instance, it would be sheerly impossible for two of us to be pulling against each other like that.'

'But, darling, I take it you haven't got two near-geniuses in your family,' retorted Oliver with a laugh. 'Father is, quite frankly, jealous of the fact that Marc has written something he couldn't do himself. – Oh, yes, he is!' as Gail made a movement of protest. 'He probably doesn't know it, and I don't think one can altogether blame him. Composing was the thing he most longed to do. But although he had most of the other gifts, he just hadn't got that.'

'Will he feel just as badly about your work too?' she asked.

'No, no. He can allow himself the luxury of despising my type of composition. Or at least treating it with good-humoured condescension.'

'Do you mind?' she said curiously.

'Not in the least. I see things as they are, not as I would wish them to be, which – as Napoleon or someone said – is the basis of being in a strong position. I and my mother are the clear-headed ones in our family—'

'Your mother?' Gail could not hide her surprise.

'Yes, of course. Oh, don't be deceived by that vague air of hers. It's just a clever pose. Something which cools down tempers and prevents explosions in a family like ours. Behind it she has each one of us summed up to perfection. She loves us all, but my father infinitely more than Marc or me.' He said that without a scrap of rancour. 'That's why she backed him up immediately when he wanted to hear you sing. She knows it soothes his pride to make decisions over everything that happens in our household.'

'Do you think,' Gail asked rather anxiously, 'that she knows about your father's plans for me?'

'I expect so. At least, she probably guesses. She is an inspired guesser. She knows it will please the old man no end if he can feel that at least he discovered and personally developed the central character. Marc may have created the work, but he will virtually have created *you*.'

They had arrived at Gail's front door by the time they came to this point in the discussion, and she paused there, curiously disturbed by the idea of being, in a sense, Quentin Bannister's creation.

'Don't look so worried,' Oliver smiled down at her in the light from a nearby street lamp. 'There are worse things for a singer to be than the creation of Quentin Bannister. It could be the beginning of a great career.'

'I know. That's why I was so tempted. But I hate the idea of Marc being – cheated, in some way.'

'Oh, let him take his chance!' Suddenly Oliver reverted to his more usual air of cheerful indifference. 'I don't know why I carried a torch so eagerly for him during the last ten minutes. Maybe I still half hoped, even now, to wean you away from your operatic plans and into our orbit. But I resign.' He caught her hands and kissed them lightly, one after the other. 'Go ahead and let Father do his best with you. Who knows? It *might* end in Marc simply loving you. In the part, of course.'

The discussion ended there, and he bade her goodnight. But the words which remained most persistently with her were his last ones. 'It might end in Marc simply loving you. In the part, of course.'

On Tuesday she still had some faint doubts what she should or would do. But Quentin Bannister's patent delight in her progress, and the absorbing interest with which he invested her whole lesson, decided her. All this weighed far more heavily in the scales then any academic doubts about justice being done to Marc.

So happy and excited were she and Quentin Bannister – and, indeed, Elsa Marburger too – that nothing in the world seemed so important as the slow, steady re-creation of what promised to be a splendid operatic figure.

'Every operatic character is dead while still on paper,' Quentin Bannister declared. 'It's like bringing someone to life to hear and see Anya like this.'

This was nothing less than the truth, of course. And the implication was warmly flattering to the work Gail was doing. But she remembered for a moment what Oliver had said, and she realized with a slight shock that the older Bannister spoke almost as though he were taking over his son's work and making it something of his own.

'I can't help it,' she told herself impatiently. 'They must settle their family differences themselves. For me this is the chance of a lifetime, and I'm taking it.'

From then on she lived, breathed, slept and lived the part of Anya. The more so as Quentin Bannister told her that there was indeed a time limit. Oliver had been right. Oscar Warrender was sufficiently interested to want to conduct the first performances himself, and he would want the first auditions taken before he left for the States in some weeks' time.

'We are setting aside two weeks for auditioning,' Quentin Bannister told her. 'And if you go on like this I have very few doubts about your getting the part, Gail. – By the way,' he smiled suddenly and produced another copy of the score, 'Marc sent you this.'

'*Marc* did?'

'Yes. There are further copies available now, of course, and they are going out to the people we want to audition. Marc was quite willing for you to be one among the several. You had better take this one now and return me my personal score.'

Slowly she made the exchange.

'Then it doesn't matter now his knowing that I'm working on the role?'

'Of course not. We just won't mention the fact that you have been doing so already for the last month,' he replied genially. 'But that extra month should put you well in the lead,' he added, with an air of considerable satisfaction.

'You're a fortunate girl,' Madame Marburger told her later, when Quentin Bannister had gone. 'Few people can have been given such intensive expert guidance for their first serious attempt at an operatic role.'

'You don't think,' said Gail, looking down at the score she was holding, 'that there's something just a bit unfair about it?'

'Unfair to whom?' Elsa Marburger raised her eyebrows. 'To your competitors, do you mean? It would be altogether too altruistic to look at it that way, Gail.' She seemed amused – as well she might be, Gail supposed. 'You have certainly been very lucky to have Mr. Bannister interest himself so personally in your progress. But luck plays a part in every career. I don't know quite what you mean by something unfair about it.'

'No – no, of course not,' Gail agreed hastily.

'Don't press your luck too far, though,' her teacher warned her brusquely. 'You will have to be supremely good, even now, to carry off the prize. You are an absolute unknown, remember – in this field particularly – and you may not be everyone's idea of Anya, so—'

'What do you mean by that?' Gail looked startled.

'Just what I say, my dear. You sing the part well, and present it with a great deal of youthful pathos and charm. Maybe that's how Marc Bannister meant it to be. But there are other ways of playing it. There always are. Particularly with an entirely new role. If you risked being less than your own particular best, and someone else offered a different, more acceptable way of doing it, your chances would be halved. So go on working hard.'

Gail went on working hard. And a week later she had a telephone call from Marc. She recognized his voice at once, and her heart gave a nervous little flutter which, oddly enough, was almost entirely pleasurable.

'Gail? I wanted to know if you are still seriously interested in auditioning for Anya?'

'But of *course* I am!' To Gail, who had thought of little else for weeks, this was so self-evident that she nearly gave herself away. Then she remembered that of course Marc had no idea how intensively she had been involving herself. 'I loved the role even on first hearing,' she explained hastily. 'Thank you very much for sending me the score. I've worked on nothing else all this week.'

That was the truth, if not the whole truth. And she heard him give a pleased laugh.

'You restore my spirits,' he told her, half seriously. 'I had just reached the point of wondering if the work was any good, after all.'

'You can't be serious!'

'More than half,' he assured her. 'One does get like that, you know, over one's own work. At one moment it seems the ultimate expression of all one wanted to say. Then suddenly you can't imagine why you ever thought it worth bothering about. But I'm encouraged by Warrender's view. He thinks it's really worthwhile, and there's no better judge alive. Though, like everyone else, naturally, he suspends final judgement until the work is off the page and on the stage, so to speak. By the way, he is going to be one of the judges at the auditions.'

Gail started to say, 'I know—' But remembering that she was not really supposed to know anything much about the progress of the whole enterprise, she hastily changed it to, 'I know you couldn't have anyone better. Have there been many applications for the part of Anya, Marc?'

'Rather more than I expected. You'll be getting particulars about the day and time when they – we – want to hear you. I just wanted to make sure that you were seriously in the running still.'

She thought, 'I'm in the lead, if you but knew it!' Then the sheer conceit of that shook her and she said humbly, 'I'm very glad to be allowed to make a stab at it.'

'Well – good luck.' He said that as he might have said it to anyone, but she prized it all the same. And when he had rung off she stood for several seconds with the receiver in her hand before she slowly replaced it.

Two days later her summons to the audition came. It was for an afternoon in about ten days' time, and there was apparently no objection to Madame Marburger coming with her, if she wished to do so.

'Of course I'll come!' Madame Marburger looked rather less than her calm, dignified self at the prospect. 'It could be an historic occasion, I suppose.' She laughed good-humouredly and patted Gail's arm. 'In any case, to hear Oscar Warrender – not to mention the two Bannisters – hold an audition is in itself something not to be missed.'

Gail was very glad of her company when the great afternoon finally came. The auditions were being held in a small practice theatre off Oxford Street, and when they made their entrance by the stage door they could already hear sounds of a tenor voice filtering through from the stage.

'That's Henry Paulton, if I'm not mistaken,' observed Madame Marburger, cocking an attentive ear. 'Wonderful character singer, although he's quite young. Very sympathetic and sensitive. I shouldn't wonder—' She broke off, as though realizing suddenly that she could hardly expect her young companion to be interested in the prospects of any mere tenor at that moment.

They were conducted by an extremely indifferent young woman into a small dressing-room, and asked to wait. Here also they could hear something of what was happening on the stage. And presently the tenor voice was succeeded by a good strong mezzo voice singing Anya's monologue from the first act.

Neither Gail nor her teacher said anything until the end. Then Madame Marburger shook her head decisively.

'It's a good voice,' Gail ventured.

'Excellent raw material,' replied Madame Marburger. 'Very raw,' she added, and Gail felt cheered.

Five minutes later the indifferent young woman looked in and said, 'If you're ready, Miss—' she consulted a list – 'Rostall.'

Miss Rostall had never felt less ready in her life. But she came. In the dusty space at the side of the stage, Quentin Bannister unexpectedly came forward to greet them. But he made rather more of Madame Marburger than her pupil. ('Just as though he hadn't seen me since that week-end in his home,' thought Gail, oddly shocked.)

'Come and sit in the body of the house, Madame Marburger,' he said courteously. 'We're very glad to have you here. And no doubt you'll prefer to hear your protégée from a good vantage point.'

So Gail was left alone, standing in the wings, and feeling indescribably lost and scared. Then Oscar Warrender's authoritative voice said from the darkened stalls, 'Miss Rostall? – Will you come on now, please. We should like to hear you sing the monologue from the first act.'

From somewhere in the shabby little orchestra pit a piano began to play, and Gail came out on to the stage. There was not a thing to help her. Nothing to create an atmosphere. Not a backdrop, not a stage prop. Nothing but a bare, dusty stage, and the yawning cavern of the darkened theatre where presumably the arbiters of her fate were sitting. In all her life she had never been so alone and scared.

Then she glanced down at the pianist and at that moment Marc leaned forward in the front row to say a word to the man at the piano. She saw him very distinctly in the unshaded light from the orchestra pit and he too looked tense and fearful. And all at once she realized that, however dreadful this was for her, it must be ten times worse for him. Over and over again he must have had to listen to his own music sung in a variety of ways, from good to very bad. The exacting and unsympathetic circumstances must have been like a butchering of all he held most dear.

Her whole heart went out to him in that moment, and instantly her nervousness left her. All she wanted was that he should hear how truly beautiful his own creation was. And she began the lovely, nostalgic, heart-searching air with all the vocal skill which Madame Marburger had taught her over the years and, it must be admitted, with all the infinitely musical phrasing and artistic tone colouring that Quentin Bannister had imparted to her over the last few weeks.

No one stopped her at any point. She was allowed to sing right through to the end. After which there was almost a minute's silence that was, she knew, an astonished tribute to her unexpected performance.

'Very beautiful,' said Quentin Bannister's voice from the darkness at last, as though he were just as surprised as everyone else. 'I congratulate you on your pupil, Madame Marburger.'

Gail did not hear what tactful words her teacher murmured in reply, for Oscar Warrender came forward into the circle of light from the stage, looked up at her and said, 'Have you studied the last act, Miss Rostall?'

'Oh, yes.'

'Miss Gregory—' he called into the wings, and the indifferent young woman – now looking rather slavish – trotted out expectantly. 'Ask Mr. Paulton to come back here if he is still in the house.'

'Yes, Mr. Warrender.' She hurried away, and there was a slight pause, while Gail was aware of a good deal of low-toned conversation going on in the body of the theatre.

Then a rather slight, youngish-looking man with an eager, intelligent face came on to the stage.

'Mr. Paulton' – that was Oscar Warrender again – 'this is Miss Rostall, who is auditioning for the part of Anya. We should like to hear her in the final scene. Would you mind joining her for the duet?'

It seemed he didn't mind at all. He smiled at Gail in a friendly way and said, 'Are we taking it from your en-

103

trance?'

'I think so.' She glanced inquiringly at the pianist, who nodded. And, quite naturally, as though she knew every move in the scene, Gail went to the back of the stage. Then, with the instinctive feeling for simple pathos which was one of her genuine gifts, she made a slow, bewildered, childlike entrance, singing her first broken phrases.

No one had really suggested that the two should act out the scene, as well as sing it. But young Paulton, who was a born stage person, immediately fell in with her mood, and together they went through to the end of the opera, giving quite a remarkable degree of acting power as well as some excellent singing.

At the end, Warrender said briefly, 'Very good – both of you.'

Quentin Bannister said, 'I would never have believed it, from a virtually unknown artist! You know, I doubt if we shall have to look much further.'

'We'll see.' Warrender frowned at the indiscretion of such frank speech in front of mere audition material. Then he turned to Marc, who had volunteered nothing so far, and asked, 'How do you feel about it, Marc?'

Gail could see him again very clearly in the light from the stage. He looked a good deal more relaxed, but he smoothed back his hair with both hands in a half nervous gesture.

'I'm not quite sure. I like it – yes, of course I like it. An incredibly musical and sensitive performance. Not quite—' Then he looked up suddenly and smiled full at Gail and said, 'My word, you must have worked hard on that!'

'I did.' Gail smiled down at him. 'And I'm simply in love with the part by now.'

'Well, we won't keep either of you any longer,' observed Warrender, evidently feeling that the talk was becoming a little too unofficial. 'We have several other people to hear in the next few days, but we will let you know if we need you here again.' He spoke a word or two to the Bannisters in an undertone, and then added, 'Will you keep next Friday afternoon clear, please.'

They both said they would. Then Gail and Henry Paulton left the stage together and he took her by the arm.

'You were simply terrific!' he told her with genuine enthusiasm. 'Why haven't I come across you before?'

'Probably because I don't really belong to the operatic world,' Gail said. 'This is the first time I've ever auditioned for an operatic role.'

'The *first time*?' He looked at her with frank incredulity. 'You can't mean it! Then you're either a God-given natural at this job, or you've been coached by a genius.'

This was so dangerously near the truth that Gail laughed nervously, quite unable to find suitable words with which to reply.

'You took the stage like a pro,' he assured her. 'And some of that phrasing was quite wonderful. Who taught you how to time those marvellous short pauses between the opening phrases?'

Who indeed?

'Well, I thought – it sounded to me—' Gail stammered into embarrassed silence. And then, to her measureless relief, Madame Marburger joined them at that moment, and she was saved from the necessity of explaining the inexplicable.

'Let's go now.' She turned eagerly to her teacher. 'I don't know why, but I just suddenly feel completely flaked out.'

'It's the strain and excitement,' Henry Paulton told her

kindly. 'The anxiety first, and then the relief of quite a remarkable success. Well, I'll be seeing you, I hope. Till Friday!' And he turned away.

Back in the small dressing-room, while she and Madame Marburger were putting on their coats, Gail had almost nothing to say. But the older woman evidently understood how she was feeling, for she made no attempt at conversation until they had left the theatre.

Then she firmly hailed a passing taxi, hustled Gail into it and, sitting down beside her said, 'Well done, Gail. You were a great deal better than I dared to hope.'

'Were you doubtful about me, then?' Gail gave her a quick, searching glance.

'Not at all. I meant that, high though my hopes were, you actually surpassed them. Frankly, any Anya who takes the part from you now will have to be very good indeed.'

'Oh, I'm so glad!' And just to show how glad she was Gail began to cry.

'Come, come—' her teacher's tone was bracing, but not unsympathetic. 'There's nothing to cry about. Very much the reverse. But you're getting a bit of nervous reaction now, I expect. I shall take you straight home. And you had better have a quiet and restful evening.'

'Yes,' Gail promised meekly. 'And I can't thank you enough for all your support.'

'Don't thank me!' The other woman laughed quietly. 'What sort of a present do you suppose this afternoon was for me too? One doesn't often have even one's best pupil seize an opportunity like this with both hands. If you get this part, my dear, I shall be just as pleased as you will.'

'And will you be terribly disappointed if I don't get it?' Gail asked, with a sort of nervous anxiety she could not quite explain to herself.

'To a certain degree – of course. Just as you will be,' Madame Marburger replied. 'But our profession is full of hopes and fears, triumphs and disappointments. One has to learn to take the one with the other. I have learned that long ago, and you will have to learn the same. If the account balances reasonably well in the end, one cannot complain.'

And, on this admirable piece of philosophy, she left Gail at her door and drove on in the taxi.

It was one thing to be told to have a quiet and restful time. It was quite another thing to carry out the advice. For several minutes after she got in, Gail just walked up and down the room, trying to quiet her nerves and balance her hopes and fears, as Madame Marburger had told her to do.

By any reckoning, it had been an afternoon of something like triumph. Oscar Warrender himself had praised her. Quentin Bannister had (with some effrontery, it must be admitted) spoken as though the role were already hers. Even Marc had praised her for the work she had done.

But then, of course, he thought he was hearing the result of a couple of weeks of unaided work. Unaided, that was to say, by anyone but her excellent singing teacher. He had no idea that what he had heard and seen that afternoon was the fine flower of his father's determined coaching. That was the thought which came to sour the sweet flavour of success.

'Oh, don't be so *silly*!' she admonished herself, even speaking aloud in the intensity of her desire to be convinced by her own arguments. 'It doesn't matter *how* you arrived at the final result. Only that you arrived there.'

An incredibly musical and sensitive performance! That

had been Marc's actual verdict. And he had said that he liked it – that 'of course' he liked it. As though there could be no second opinion about that.

But his very first words, when Oscar Warrender had appealed to him for his opinion, had been, 'I'm not quite sure—'

And that, Gail knew to the bottom of her soul, exactly described his genuine state of mind. He had no idea what had brought him to that point. He only knew that something intrinsically good had confused the issue for him with regard to his own creation.

She was so shocked by the acceptance of this thought that when the telephone rang at her elbow she jumped as though she had been shot.

It must be Marc! Her own guilty thoughts convinced her of that. And her heart was thumping and her hand trembling as she took up the receiver.

But it was Oliver's gay, reassuring voice which said, 'Hello, Gail! How did you get on? It *was* the audition this afternoon, wasn't it?'

'Yes. Yes, it was. And I got on—' she swallowed nervously – 'pretty well.'

'Only pretty well?' He said that kindly, but with the true professional's desire for exact information.

'Well, Warrender said I was very good and—'

'Warrender did?' Oliver whistled appreciatively. 'Those were his exact words? Then you must have done better than pretty well, my dear. He's very sparing with his praise at the best of times. And at an audition he's a regular old oyster. I take it Father gave a splendid performance of being as surprised as everyone else?'

'Yes, he did. It made me feel guilty, somehow. Well, not exactly *guilty*—' as there was a derisive sound of protest from Oliver. 'But oh, it would have been so much,

much nicer if everyone there had known the simple truth that your father was largely responsible for my being so satisfactory in the part. It all seemed so silly and un-neccessary, this elaborate deception.'

'It won't, once everyone is satisfied that you are the right person to have the part,' Oliver assured her soothingly. 'How did Marc react?'

'Favourably, on the whole,' Gail said slowly. 'I'd done the final scene with Henry Paulton – who is quite mar-vellous, by the way—'

'I know. I've always admired him.'

'—And then Mr. Warrender said we were both very good, and he turned to Marc and asked what he thought. And although Marc praised us too, his first words were, "I'm not quite sure—"'

'Were they indeed?' Suddenly Oliver sounded amused, and even a trifle smug.

'I don't know what's so pleasing about that!' she ex-claimed with unexpected irritation.

'I was just congratulating myself on being so right about my own family,' he replied rather complacently.

'Yes, you were quite right, weren't_you?' Gail spoke quietly and very deliberately. 'Marc knew the per-formance was intrinsically good. But it wasn't *his* idea of the part. However, it was so good—' she stated that with-out conceit or false modesty – 'that he was actually con-fused in his own mind about what he really wanted. Your father had successfully superimposed his idea of Anya on top of Marc's theoretical conception of the part. *That's* what makes me feel guilty about the work we've done together. And I'm not withdrawing the word this time.'

'Don't exaggerate things, darling—' Oliver began, again in that soothing tone he had used before.

But, before he could get any further, she said sharply, 'I can't talk about it any more, Oliver. It upsets me too much.' And she abruptly replaced the receiver.

Within a couple of minutes the telephone rang again.

So unwilling was she to continue the conversation that she wanted just to ignore the shrill sound. But it persisted and, knowing Oliver was perfectly well aware that she was there, she finally snatched up the receiver again and said breathlessly, 'I'm sorry. But I just can't—'

'Gail, is that you?' Marc's voice cut across her words.

'Oh – oh, yes,' she stammered. 'I thought it was – someone else.'

'Were you expecting a call? Would you like me to ring off?'

'No, no!' Scared though she had been ten minutes ago at the very thought of speaking to him, now, she realized, the last thing she wanted him to do was to ring off again. 'What is it, Marc?'

'First of all, I want to congratulate you on your performance this afternoon. It was quite stunning, in its way. I want to talk to you about it. Will you come out and have dinner with me?'

'This evening, do you mean?' Part of her was enraptured at the thought. But her fears made her prevaricate. 'I'm rather tired, really. And – and—'

'Yes, I know. It must have been a wearing afternoon for you. It was for me too, to tell the truth. We'll go somewhere quiet, and just discuss Anya. Unless you're sick of the subject. How about it, Gail?'

'I'd like to,' she said slowly. And then, on an impulse she couldn't control, 'Marc, tell me something. Did you really like my Anya?' There was a moment of hesitation before he replied, 'Yes. I liked it.'

'But it just isn't *your* idea of Anya at all, is it?'

This time the hesitation was a little longer. Then he said, 'No, Gail, it isn't. But maybe I'm wrong. That's why I must talk to you about it.'

CHAPTER SIX

MORE than once during the hour or so before Marc came to take her out to dinner, Gail was tempted to telephone again and say that she could not come, after all. But, each time, her desire to go was just a bit stronger than her fear of the consequences. And so, when he arrived at seven o'clock, she was ready and waiting for him.

She looked from the window when the bell rang and saw that he was driving the car in which he had fetched her and Oliver from the station, that very first day. And, as she ran downstairs to join him, she could not help thinking how dramatically her life had changed since that day.

Her view of Marc had changed a good deal too. Not only because she had met him and talked with him since, but because it was not possible to have studied his work so intensively without gaining some knowledge of the sensitivity, the feeling for beauty, the real compassion and the deep human warmth which his music revealed.

'I feel rather guilty to be dragging you out when you're tired.' He smiled at her as she got into the seat beside him. 'But I must say you look remarkably fresh and charming for an exhausted girl.'

She laughed and said that she had had time to rest and was now ready to enjoy herself.

'It must have been a lot worse for you,' she declared as they drove away from the house. 'To hear your own work given rough, smooth or sheerly brutal treatment over and over again, before a critical audience, must have been sheer murder.'

'It was,' he assured her. But he seemed able to smile about it now, all the same.

'Just before I began – when I was feeling at my very worst – I caught a glimpse of you in the light from the stage,' she told him. 'You looked very much as *I* was feeling, and I realized suddenly that it must be ten times worse for you. While I was feeling sorry for you I somehow didn't feel so frightful about myself. It steadied me quite a bit.'

'Was that why you sang so beautifully?'

'I suppose it was. If I did sing beautifully.'

'You did, Gail. In fact, quite a lot of your performance would not have disgraced the most accomplished artist. I had no idea that you truly knew so much about your job. I completely underestimated you that time I first heard you. And I'm prepared to admit it now.'

'Oh—' she said, and cleared her throat nervously. Then after that she was silent. Partly because she was greatly moved by his generous admission. Partly because she wondered, rather panic-stricken, how long it would be before she somehow let slip the fact that someone other than herself was chiefly responsible for that incredibly mature performance.

He appeared to find nothing unusual in her silence, probably putting it down to the fact that she was, admittedly, tired and willing to take things lazily. Indeed, not until they were established at a secluded table in a small, quiet and elegant restaurant did he revert to the subject of the audition again. And then only after he had consulted her about her exact tastes in food and drink.

Then, as they sipped their aperitifs, he asked – not searchingly, more in a tone of friendly curiosity, 'How did you come to be so completely at home in that role in so short a time, Gail? Had you thought about it a great deal between your visit down home and your first getting the score two weeks ago?'

'Yes, of course.' That at least was strictly true. 'I was fascinated by the work, and particularly by Anya's music, from the first time I heard it at your home. Her character is so appealing, so—'

'Is that how she seems to you?' he interrupted. 'You really think of her as young – touching – appealing? A sort of little-girl-lost?'

'Y-yes, I think I do. Don't you?'

'Not at all.' He shook his head. 'I suppose that was why I was taken aback by your performance, as well as tremendously impressed by it.'

'Tell me how you see her,' said Gail rather timidly.

'To me she is a typical woman from central or eastern Europe. Rather earthy. Almost peasant-like. Neither understanding nor liking much of what she sees around her in her new country. She's lost, it's true, in the deepest sense of the term. That's why she bruises herself against every new and unexpected experience. But she is *strong*, in a primitive way. After all, she was sufficiently single-minded to go with her man into what was, for her, the unknown. That he abandons her there is her tragedy. But one is left, in that last scene, with the feeling that she will somehow rise above the tragedy, because she is basically strong and beautiful. I wrote her music with that type of woman in mind. It seems to me that what I wrote expresses her like that.'

'Then you mean,' said Gail, after a pause, 'that my conception of the part is wrong? that, left to yourself, you would not be in favour of casting me for Anya?'

'If I'd simply heard about your conception of the part in theory, quite frankly, I wouldn't. But you gave such an amazingly complete performance of what you conceive to be the part that, to tell you the truth, I'm shaken. To arrive at such a finished, "in-depth" idea of the girl in a matter of two weeks can mean only that you were pretty well inspired. I don't think I've ever known such a thing happen before.'

'You – you mean that?' He was not the only one who was shaken at that point.

'Yes, I do.' Marc looked across the table at her with a sort of admiring curiosity. 'It's an extraordinary experience, to be given an entirely new slant on a creation of one's own by a slip of a girl like you. It's not only that you obviously *feel* Anya that way. Everything is musically geared to the idea. Phrasing, balance, tone-colour. It's an amazing achievement. Would be amazing in an experienced artist. In a girl like you it's almost frightening.'

'Oh, no!' protested Gail, who felt much more frightened than he possibly could have in that moment.

'Well, at least it gives one a terrific mental jolt,' he declared. 'That's why I've spent the last few hours asking myself if a mere composer could perhaps be wrong about his own work.'

He laughed as he said that, but his eyes were serious as they regarded her, still with that air of puzzled interest.

'Perhaps,' suggested Gail desperately, 'someone else will come along with *your* idea of the part magnificently carried out. Then you'll know that you were right, and that she is the person for the part.'

'Very high-minded of you to say so,' he said teasingly. 'But the fact is, my dear, that you were the last one we auditioned for the part of Anya. The remaining auditions are for the men.'

'I was the last one?' Suddenly her eyes were wide, and her heart was beating hard.

'Yes. I intended you to be heard earlier on and, quite

candidly, cleared out of the way with several other (as I thought) inconsiderable applicants. It was my father who, for some unknown reason, had you moved to the end of the list.'

'Was it?' said Gail faintly, and she passed the tip of her tongue over rather dry lips. 'And among those you heard before me, were there none who handled the role in the way you see it?'

'One or two of them – yes. In a strictly conventional operatic sort of way. But none of them displayed your artistry or originality. One well-known singer – I won't name her – had a good idea of the part, but the voice is thinning out badly nowadays, because she has been doing roles that are much too heavy for her. On the other hand, the girl just before you, for instance, had a splendid voice and a certain feeling for drama. But she was pretty raw stuff, really.'

Gail remembered that Madame Marburger had used just that term, but she said doubtfully, 'You don't think you could work on her? Refine her performance in some way?'

'No,' replied Marc, without qualification. And Gail nervously tasted the delicious food set in front of her and said nothing.

'The second girl we auditioned had something of my idea of Anya, and I thought she might be teachable. But my father turned her down unhesitatingly. And, though I don't see eye to eye with him about everything, I have to accept his judgement on that particular topic. He has an infallible talent for knowing just what an artist should sound like if properly handled. When he says there is potential there, he's invariably right. When he says not, then I'm bound to say one has to accept it.'

'I see,' said Gail, feeling worse and worse. Then presently, after a great effort to calm herself, she managed to ask, 'Are you still trying to make up your own mind? or have you really come to some sort of decision, and are just wondering how to carry the others with you?'

'I've almost come to a decision, Gail. And that would mean my letting the others carry *me* with *them*,' he admitted with a laugh. 'The fact is that your performance was so gloriously right, on its own terms, that I'm inclined to accept it, even though it isn't my own original conception of the part.'

'But you don't feel altogether happy about it?'

'If anyone else of real quality were in the running, I'd be less able to make up my mind. As it is—' he paused, bit his lip, and then suddenly seemed to come to a decision – 'as it is, Gail, your performance is too good to turn down. I accept it.'

For a moment Gail knew exactly what was meant when people spoke of 'the room whirling round them'. She was literally giddy. Then she put her hand over Marc's as it lay on the table and said earnestly, 'Marc, will you try to teach me your idea of Anya?'

'No, darling.' He seemed quite unaware that he had called her 'darling', but to her the word seemed to hang in the air in letters of gold. 'To try to change your basic idea of the part would be absolutely fatal. Besides, everything about you is natural to the way you play it. You aren't a strong, primitive, earthy character. You *are* the appealing "little-girl-lost" type. At least, when you sing, you are,' he added apologetically as she made a sound of rather disgusted dissent.

Indeed, she made a movement to draw her hand away, only he turned his and held her fingers strongly.

'Let's have champagne,' he exclaimed, and suddenly he shed all his doubts and anxieties and, for the first time since she had known him, looked faintly like Oliver in his unexpected gaiety. 'This is an occasion, if ever there was one. I know Warrender would have a fit if he knew you and I were already drinking to the fact that the part is yours. But I can't help knowing that they are all in favour of you. Now I'm in favour of you also. And there is no one else to audition. So let's drink to your success as Anya — and hang the auditioning formalities.'

She laughed in purest joy and relief, and in that moment she could have leant across the table and kissed him.

This was how Oliver had said it might be — if all went well. She need never worry again about Quentin Bannister's little deception beforehand. His methods — though questionable — had justified themselves. Marc had seen nothing but the finished product — and he was satisfied. Or nearly so.

As she drank the champagne with Marc, and laughed in her happiness and relief, she found herself almost blurting out the whole secret of why she had shown up so wonderfully at the audition. Indeed, only her promise to the older Bannister kept her silent.

Later, when she thought it over, she decided it was the champagne which had made her even entertain such a mad idea. For of course, even when — or if — Marc had to know the whole story, he would find it hard to take the fact that his father had interfered in such an arbitrary manner in his affairs.

'I'll wait until after the first night,' Gail thought dreamily. 'I'll wait until the work has proved itself — and I have proved *my*self. Then nothing will matter. Nothing but the fact that Marc will know I have helped to make his opera a success. And perhaps he will love me a little for that.'

This final conclusion came to her only after he had taken her home and, still in a golden haze of happiness, she was reviewing their evening together.

'Do I want him to love me a little?' she asked herself, standing in front of the mirror and smiling at her own reflection.

'No. I want him to love me a *lot*!'

And then she decided that she really had had too much champagne, and she went to bed.

The next day was Tuesday, and she went to her lesson wondering very much if Quentin Bannister would turn up. And if so, how frank he would be about the result of the auditions.

Not only did he turn up, but he brought his wife with him, much to Gail's surprise and a little to Madame Marburger's annoyance. However, she hid the fact with much tact and graciousness. And, in her turn, Mrs. Bannister stayed quietly in the background until her husband asked frankly for her opinion.

'She's very good indeed, and a credit to both of you,' replied Mrs. Bannister, smiling upon all three of them with splendid impartiality. 'Is she going to have the part?'

Madame Marburger drew in her breath slightly at what she regarded as the dropping of a professional brick, for in her view one did not casually bandy about such talk until decisions had been made at top level.

Quentin Bannister, however, merely laughed indulgently and looked at Gail as though he were Jove about to lean from Olympus and bestow a godlike gift on a mere mortal. He was enjoying the moment to the full, she saw, and she was not at all sure that he had not arranged the whole thing beforehand with his wife. At any rate, she realized, it would never do to steal his thunder by letting him know that Marc had already prepared her. With hardly any effort, she brought a look of breathless expectancy to her face.

'Well, one isn't supposed to give away secrets of that sort, eh, Madame Marburger?' Jove's genial smile took in Gail's teacher also at that moment. 'But perhaps there's no harm in telling you that, so far, no applicant has pleased us all so much.'

'Thank you,' murmured Gail, dropping her glance.

'And there are no others to come,' he finished with a laugh. Then, as Gail looked up quickly, he added warningly, 'But on Friday, when Warrender tells you that the part is yours, you will oblige me by looking extremely surprised.'

'Oh, I will, I will!' Gail promised. Then she came to him and took his outstretched hand. 'And I can never, never thank you enough, Mr. Bannister, for all you have done for me.'

'It was nothing – nothing,' he said, not meaning that at all, of course. 'If you hadn't been an extremely gifted, hard-working girl I wouldn't have raised a finger for you.' And that he did mean. 'Anyway, I must go now. Don't stop working just because the goal is in sight. There's a great deal still between you and final success. The audition is only the first – though perhaps the worst – hurdle.'

Gail promised earnestly to work as hard as ever. Then Quentin Bannister went away to some meeting he had to attend and Gail, having exchanged a jubilant glance with her teacher and promised to telephone later that day, went out into the street with Mrs. Bannister.

As they walked together towards Oxford Street, Mrs. Bannister said, 'I'm very happy about this, Gail. And very grateful to you.'

'*Grateful*, Mrs. Bannister? Why, the gratitude is all on my side, so far as your family is concerned.'

'No, not entirely. There could have been a great deal of friction and ill-will between Marc and his father over this opera, in certain circumstances. As it is, you seem to have found some sort of compromise which satisfies them both.'

'You were afraid that – that Mr. Bannister might be made to feel hurt and slighted?' Gail ventured.

'That – certainly,' Mrs. Bannister said, smiling slightly. 'Like all childlike people, he is curiously defenceless where his self-esteem is concerned. But Marc too, in spite of his rather arrogant air of self-sufficiency, is vulnerable. With him it is almost entirely a matter of his work. His first great triumph was ruined for him by Lena Dorman. Which is why I hate her and wish her ill,' she added casually.

'Do you?' said Gail, slightly awed, as many people had been before her, by the way Daisy Bannister could utter quite violent sentiments in that lovely caressing voice of hers.

'Of course. But she is unimportant now. What matters now is that Marc's joy in his opera should not be clouded. Unexpectedly, he and his father are at one over it, and the family harmony is undisturbed. I am a great believer in harmony in a family.'

And, on this unexceptionable statement of principle, she lightly kissed Gail's cheek and parted from her.

A good deal amused and somewhat intrigued by this further glimpse into the lives of the Bannisters, Gail went on her way – and almost immediately came face to face with Tom Mallender. But a Tom Mallender so wrapped away in his own thoughts that he would have passed her if she had not put out her hand and stopped him.

'Hey, Tom! What are you doing, cutting me dead like that?'

'Gail!' He kissed her unexpectedly. 'The very girl! Come and have tea or a drink or something. I must talk to someone. Someone who'll convince me that I'm walking on real pavements and not on clouds of my own invention.'

'This will do.' Gail took him by the arm and led him into a coffee bar, where they found a table at the back, away from most of the other people.

'Double whisky,' he said absently to the girl who came to take their order.

'This is a coffee bar,' Gail informed him. 'Bring him a very strong black coffee, and me a reasonably strong white one, please.' Then she turned to Tom and asked, 'What has happened?'

'I've just had lunch with Reuben Arrowmead.' Tom looked at her as though he hardly saw her.

'Have you?' Gail said encouragingly. 'Who is he?'

'Who *is* he? Where have you been in the last eighteen months, girl? He's one of the biggest names in the theatre world. He—'

'Oh, you mean J. R. Arrowmead. Why do you call him Reuben?'

'Because that's what his friends call him.' Tom smiled beatifically at her. ' "Call me Reuben, boy," he said. "That's what my friends call me." I'm a friend – of Reuben Arrowmead.'

'Tom, you're not drunk, are you?' Gail regarded him rather anxiously.

'Certainly not! I only had half a glass of Niersteiner with my lunch. I was too busy talking to eat or drink much. Too happy too. If I seem intoxicated it's just that I'm drunk with success.'

The black coffee came just then and he gulped half of it down and said, 'That's better. I know now that it really did happen. Isn't it the most glorious, incredible, wonderful thing ever? Haven't you got anything to say about it?'

'Not until I know what we're talking about,' Gail told him patiently. 'So far, all I know is that you had lunch with J. R. Arrowmead, and that you couldn't eat or drink much.'

'But I *told* you! — Or didn't I tell you? Lord, I don't really know what I'm doing or saying.' Tom buried his face in his hands, and his words came out in a sort of muffled rush. 'It's happened, Gail! He thinks — *Reuben Arrowmead* thinks — that a lot of what Noll and I have done is wonderful. That was his word. Wonderful! Two or three things he says won't do. We're to make changes, of course, and add various numbers under his direction. But he says we seem to have an almost inexhaustible flow of what people want. And he should know — he should know!'

'Tom, dear, but how marvellous! I can't believe it!' She leant over and gave him a kiss of uninhibited joy and congratulation. 'Do you mean that he's going to back you or something?'

'He's going to put on the show.' Tom raised his head and she saw he was genuinely pale with excitement and his eyes glittered feverishly. 'Oh, there are all sorts of details to settle yet, of course. He wouldn't even say which of his theatres he had in mind. Maybe he didn't know himself. It depends on the length of run of whatever is on at the moment. But, roughly speaking, he is thinking ahead to, say, March or April of next year.'

'I can't — believe it,' Gail said again, and she stared back at Tom.

'Nor can I. That's why I had to tell you about it. I keep on thinking I'll wake up. This isn't a dream, is it, Gail? Pinch me, just in case.'

Smilingly, she gave his arm a smart little nip and he said, 'Ouch! Well, that's real enough. Gail, we're made if the show goes on under his management. Noll and I are made. And you could be too, you silly girl, if you hadn't turned down our offer,' he added, sounding now much more like himself.

'I'm so very sorry, but—'

'You want to change your mind? You can, if you like, you know. Noll and I are big-hearted fellows. We wouldn't hold it against you that you once turned us down. How about it?'

'I can't, Tom dear. I'm an opera girl. Remember?'

'Opera!' he retorted on a note of indulgent derision. 'Who wants opera?'

'Quite a lot of people, as it happens.'

'And what are the prospects now, may I ask?' He looked at her with a sort of affectionate scorn.

'I've possibly got the lead in Marc Bannister's new opera. It isn't quite settled yet, but I've every reason to think—'

'You're backing the wrong Bannister, sweetheart. Take it from me – Oliver is the one who is going to the top.'

'I hope he is. I truly hope so. And I'll be in the front row on the first night, cheering you both to the echo,' Gail promised. 'I *know* you're made for success. Both of you. And I'm grateful for your repeated offer. Thank you, dear Tom. But my heart is elsewhere.'

'With Marc Bannister, in fact?' He glanced at her quizzically.

'With my big operatic chance,' she retorted quickly.

'Well, I admire a girl who knows her own mind so thoroughly,' he conceded with a laugh. 'Bless you, and may the whole Board of Covent Garden fall flat at your feet.'

'Improbable. But a charming thought.' Gail laughed in her turn. 'Where's Oliver, by the way? Was he at the famous lunch too?'

'Of course. He's gone home to write the hit number of the show. There are the Bannisters for you! Never let the grass grow under their feet. I'm really on my way home too—' he glanced at his watch and seemed astonished at what he saw there. 'I say! I must go.'

He paid for the coffees and they went out into the crowded street together. He kissed her once more – again without quite realizing that he was doing so, she thought, and bade her good-bye.

All the way home in the Tube train Gail had difficulty in keeping herself from smiling broadly at everything and everyone. When she was not savouring her own happiness afresh, she was thinking of the impending triumph – or so she hoped – of Oliver and Tom Mallender. It was extraordinary how one could go on for weeks and months, quite happily but with nothing very sensational happening. And then, suddenly – Wham! – the rockets of excitement and joy shot up into the sky, and the golden stars were falling all around one.

She thought the days of that week would never pass. But the longed-for Friday came at last and, once more accompanied by Madame Marburger, she went to the audition theatre.

They were early, and they slipped into the back of the auditorium, to hear the excellent baritone who was being tried out for the part of Anya's lover. Sitting there in the dark, Gail relaxed happily, able to enjoy herself, able to listen sympathetically to the efforts of others. She had come successfully through *her* ordeal. Although it was still supposed to be such a secret, she knew – and Madame Marburger knew – that the part of Anya was hers. She could afford to relax and enjoy the music for its own sake.

Ten minutes after they had come in, Quentin Bannister – who had been walking rather restlessly up and down the side gangway – saw them and came over to them.

'Oh, I'm glad you are early.' He was not, Gail saw, in a very good temper. 'Something rather tiresome and ridiculous has happened, and I'm afraid it will mean a slight delay. As you know, the auditions for Anya had been completed and the decision virtually made. But someone else has turned up – a Polish singer – and Marc and Warrender seem to think we ought to hear her.'

'Well, there wasn't exactly a time limit for applications, was there?' Madame Marburger said with remarkable self-control. 'I mean, you are auditioning to find the right artist for a role, not running a competition with rules and regulations.'

'Very true, very true,' agreed Quentin Bannister irritably. 'But one has to draw the line somewhere.'

'How was it that she came so late?' asked Gail, trying hard to sound as self-controlled as her teacher.

'She was in Germany, and only heard about the auditions by chance. As a matter of fact, Lena Dorman sent her. With an introductory letter and a strong recommendation. I should have thought,' he added disagreeably, 'that that would have been enough in itself to put Marc off.'

'Why?' inquired Madame Marburger calmly. But he pretended not to hear her.

'Anyway, it shouldn't take long to dispose of her. Here she comes,' said Quentin Bannister.

And, as he turned to go back to his seat near the front of the theatre, a thin, dark-haired girl came on to the empty stage. She was pale and nothing much to look at, and she was really rather shabbily dressed, with what looked like a dark scarf hung awkwardly over her arm.

Apparently she had some difficulty in understanding English, because when Oscar Warrender was speaking to her she twice said, 'Please?' in a foreign sort of way, and he had to repeat himself.

The pianist started the familiar opening phrases leading to Anya's monologue, and the girl took what now could be seen to be a shawl from her arm and flung it round her thin shoulders. She drew it about her, glanced round like a half-frightened animal finding itself in a strange place, and began to sing. Half to herself at first and then, as the passion of her misery and loneliness grew upon her, the tones of her truly remarkable voice warmed and darkened.

It was difficult to say at which point she ceased singing just as Anya. One only knew presently that she was singing for all the people of the world who had been torn from their proper moorings and cast upon the troubled waters of an alien existence. She was homesick longing personified. And the fact that she was not specially attractive made her all the more heartbreaking.

Gail felt her throat tighten unbearably. And it was not just fear and anxiety which drew a band round it. At the end, she forced herself to glance at her teacher, and for the first time since she had known that dignified and self-controlled woman, she saw two tears tremble on her lashes.

'She is wonderful,' Gail said simply.

'She has an impossibly strong foreign accent,' retorted

Madame Marburger, as though defensively.

'What matter? Anya is, above all things, an alien – a foreigner in a foreign land.'

Madame Marburger said nothing to that, and C. turned back to the stage to see that the baritone had been recalled, and that Warrender was asking them to do the big 'showdown' scene, as Gail always called it to herself. The scene where Anya discovered that the man for whom she had torn herself from home and country was determined to desert her.

For Gail this was always the most difficult scene of all, for it called for much more than pathos and appeal. In her heart, she sometimes thought, 'I don't know what I would do in such circumstances. I just don't know.'

But the Polish girl knew all right.

At first she was quite quiet, as though unable to make herself understand what he was saying to her. Then, when the terrible truth could be held off no longer, she began to twist her thin, rather red hands, as she broke into awkward, heartbreaking appeal. Finally, even her desperate dignity dropped from her and she turned on him, like an animal who knew that the trap had finally closed, and there poured from her a stream of rage and anguish and despair that stopped one's heart.

They were exactly the same notes that Gail herself had sung again and again – appealingly and with great pathos – but they sounded like something quite different now. They were not strictly as well sung, but they stabbed to the very centre of one's consciousness.

Quietly and as though she could not help herself, Gail rose and went silently down the gangway until she could see the faces of the men who were sitting there watching the Polish girl. There was really only one face she wanted to see. Later would be soon enough to know what Oscar

Warrender and Quentin Bannister thought. Just now only Marc's reaction mattered.

And then she caught sight of him. His face was pale and strained, his wide, fascinated gaze fixed on the Polish girl with almost agonized intensity. There was simply no doubt about it. He was watching Anya as he had visualized her.

CHAPTER SEVEN

'THANK you very much,' Gail heard Oscar Warrender say to the Polish girl, who stood there now on the bare stage looking as though she scarcely knew where she was. With a slight start Gail also seemed to come out of a sort of trance, and hastily returned to her seat at the back of the theatre.

As she sank down again beside her singing teacher, Madame Marburger said softly but urgently, 'Stay where you are. If Mr. Warrender doesn't notice us, we might manage to hear—'

She left the sentence uncompleted, and Gail realized that Oscar Warrender was speaking to the Polish girl again, this time in German, which she evidently understood much better than English. She came forward to the edge of the stage to answer him and for the first time a smile passed over her thin face.

'He is telling her they may want to hear her again tomorrow,' Madame Marburger translated in a whisper, though Gail's German was good enough for her to follow fairly easily. 'But he's sending her away now. He wants her out of the way, I suppose, while they discuss this new development.'

Her words were a tacit admission that the unexpected appearance of this newcomer had altered Gail's prospects drastically. They had come that afternoon expecting to hear that the part was Gail's. But the fact that Madame Marburger took it for granted there would be further discussion showed how good she considered the new girl to be.

If she expected any protest from Gail, none was forthcoming. It was from Quentin Bannister that the protest came, and then only when the Polish girl had left the stage. But it was voiced so clearly and emphatically that both Gail and Madame Marburger heard every word of it in the back row.

'Do we really have to go through the motions of hearing her a second time?' he said, with an irritated little laugh, calculated to minimize the effect of the girl's performance. 'We had already made up our minds. We only auditioned her out of courtesy.'

'On the contrary, we auditioned her because we wanted to hear what she could do with the part,' retorted Oscar Warrender disagreeably.

'Well, in my view, she is much too heavy,' stated the older Bannister firmly. 'She's not my idea of Anya at all.'

'The point is – is she Marc's idea of Anya?' replied the conductor. 'How about it, Marc?'

Gail bent her head and stared at her hands which were tightly clasped in her lap, and it seemed to her that what was really just a moment's pause dragged on for minutes. Then she heard Marc's voice, a trifle thick and hoarse, say, 'We had virtually cast the part already. My father is right. I don't see how we could take it away from Gail Rostall now.'

On a sudden impulse, Gail gripped her teacher's arm and whispered fiercely, 'There's a side door. Let's slip out. We can't listen to any more. Please – please—'

They rose silently and, with no more than a slight click of the bar which held the door, they were out in the street.

'We can't just run away,' Madame Marburger protested, once they were outside. 'We have been specifically summoned to a second audition.'

'We'll walk around and then go in by the front entrance in a few minutes' time.' Gail looked so pale and determined that there was no gainsaying her. 'We can apologize for being a little late if anyone says anything. But I don't think they will. They – they have other things to think about.'

'Mr. Bannister knows we were already there.'

'Oh, he doesn't matter!' Gail dismissed him ungratefully and rather disrespectfully.

They walked up and down for a few minutes. Then they went into the theatre by way of the shabby front entrance. And there, in what had once been the vestibule, they found Henry Paulton examining some flyblown notices.

'Hello,' he said. 'There seems to be quite a discussion going on in there. I thought I'd better make myself scarce, even though we're running a bit over time.'

'We thought we'd better wait too.' Gail smiled and spoke quite calmly. 'We were at the back of the auditorium, as a matter of fact. But we slipped out and decided to make another entrance.'

'What happened?' Henry Paulton looked at her curiously.

'They auditioned a Polish girl for Anya, and she was simply stunning,' Gail stated without hesitation. 'Frankly, I don't think I have much chance of the role now.'

'You can't mean it!' His protest was so obviously genuine that it warmed her heart a little. 'Why, you're just about as good as it's possible to be,' he asserted confidently. 'In what way could this girl possibly be better? Who is she, anyway? What's her name?'

'I don't know,' said Gail, answering the last question first.

'I think Oscar Warrender called her something like "Miss Spolianska!",' put in Madame Marburger.

'Oh?' Henry Paulton frowned thoughtfully. 'Yes – yes – Greta Spolianska. No, that's not the name. Erna! Erna Spolianska. She's half German and half Polish. I heard about her when I was in Germany last year. She wasn't described to me as the absolute tops. Just a good sound singer with a possible future.'

'Well, she's a good, sound singer with a probable present, if you ask me.' Gail managed to laugh faintly. 'She might not be right for everything. But she just *is* Anya.'

'I find that hard to believe. From all accounts, she isn't in the least like you.'

'Oh, no! Not in the least. She plays it quite differently. But she – she tears at your heart-strings. I know that's a silly, over-worked phrase, but it applies in this case. She gives a performance that *hurts*.'

'Well – I suppose – she might,' said Henry Paulton slowly. 'I remember now. Someone told me she was born in a camp for displaced persons.'

'Ah—' said Elsa Marburger softly. And just then a door into the auditorium was thrust open and Quentin Bannister came out, blinking slightly in the sudden sunlight.

'Oh, there you are!' he exclaimed irritably. 'Why are you hanging about here? You were supposed to be in the theatre a quarter of an hour ago.'

'We thought,' replied Madame Marburger smoothly, 'that it was more seemly for us to make ourselves scarce while you were all discussing Miss Spolianska.' And no one could have guessed from her polite explanation that, but for Gail, she would have done her best to stay and hear the vital discussion.

'Well—' began Quentin Bannnister. 'Well, that was

very discreet and proper, I'm sure. But the discussion is over. We all want to hear Gail and Henry again, as was originally intended.'

'You – you want to hear me again?' stammered Gail, her precarious calm deserting her and her anxiety showing in face and voice.

'But of course.' Quentin Bannister put his hand round her arm and said reassuringly, 'Don't worry, my dear child. Effective though that girl was, it's you who will be getting the part.'

For a moment hope flared up in her heart.

'How do you know?' she whispered urgently. 'Mr. Warrender said you all wanted to hear her again tomorrow.'

'If we do give her a second hearing, instead of phoning to say the role has already been cast, we should only be going through the necessary motions,' he declared airily. 'Both Marc and I are quite decided—'

'Marc!' she interrupted almost violently. '*Marc* wants me for Anya?'

'Of course, of course. Marc has very good judgment, when it comes to the point,' said Marc's father generously.

'Did he *say* he wanted me?'

'Certainly he said so. You don't have to be afraid of Marc.'

'I'm not afraid of Marc,' she said, almost to herself. 'I'm afraid *for* him.'

Quentin Bannister glanced at her quickly. But if he had any doubts on that he stifled them.

'Marc feels – exactly as I do – that the part was virtually yours already. It was a mistake even to hear anyone else at this point. It only confuses the issue about the proper interpretation of the role. You had been as good as told that the part was yours. As Marc said, it would be grossly unfair to you, as well as detrimental to the performance, to make a change now.'

'And Mr. Warrender? What did Oscar Warrender say?'

'My dear—' Quentin Bannister made a humorous little grimace of protest – 'it's not my business to report the exact exchange of opinions to you. And it's certainly not your business to ask. Come along now and let us hear you and Henry again. What you will finally be told will be the majority opinion. And that's all that concerns you.'

So she went back into the theatre, where she and Henry Paulton went through a good deal of their part again. And presently she was called on to do the famous scene with the baritone. The one in which Erna Spolianska had been so overwhelming.

Gail did her very best. She determinedly blanked off that part of her mind which kept on recalling the way Marc had looked when he had been listening to the Polish girl. And because she was, in actual fact, afraid that her dearest wish might even now be snatched away from her, she did give an extraordinarily moving impression of someone fighting desperately to retain all that she held most dear.

It was the best she had ever done in this scene, she knew. But, even so, it seemed to her that her performance must be a pale thing in comparison with the Polish girl's riveting presentation of the part. And at the end she was limp and distressed.

Then Marc smiled up at her, which suddenly made her want to cry. And Quentin Bannister leaned forward and said something in a smiling undertone to Warrender.

He received no answering smile. Warrender merely listened and then turned to Marc. There was a vigorous, low-toned conversation between the two, ending with a shrug on the conductor's part. Then Warrender stood up and addressed Gail and the baritone.

'You will be hearing from us – both of you – by letter,' he said. And the final audition was over.

'Really, they might have given us some sort of hint,' the baritone remarked to Gail with an angry little laugh when they were in the wings again. 'I don't know why they need to keep us on tenterhooks any longer. Gives them a feeling of power, I suspect. Warrender particularly.'

'I don't think it's intentional,' said Gail wearily. 'I think there is genuinely a sharp division of opinion. About me – not you.'

'You're too modest,' declared the baritone, but she thought he found her explanation acceptable. 'Well, I suppose we shall have to chew our finger-ends a little longer.'

But it seemed that Marc was determined that Gail at least should not be left any longer in agonizing doubt. He caught up with her just as she was going into her dressing-room, and before Madame Marburger had come round to join her.

'It's all right, Gail dear,' he said. 'I don't intend to have you harrowed any more. The part is yours.'

'You shouldn't tell me!' Suddenly there were tears in her eyes. 'You can't really know. Anything could happen.'

'It's my opera, isn't it?' He spoke almost defensively.

'Yes, but—' she stopped. And then she said doggedly, 'That Polish girl was marvellous. Don't you think so?'

'Yes. But I think you're marvellous too,' he replied lightly. And then Madame Marburger came into sight at the end of the corridor, and Marc whispered quickly,

'Don't tell anyone else yet, though. It's just between you and me.'

'Yes, of course,' Gail promised, and he was gone.

'I have an appointment, Gail, and I must leave you now,' her teacher said as she came up. 'Try not to worry too much. You have done your very best and no one can do more.'

'I'll try,' Gail said, and she managed to smile almost naturally, because she was so relieved to be left alone and not to have to make conversation any longer.

The events of the afternoon had followed so quickly and relentlessly upon each other that she had had no time to think of their significance. Still less their implications. But now, left alone, she sat down on one of the hard wooden chairs, leant her elbow on the wide shelf which did duty as a dressing-table, and tried to go slowly and constructively over all that had happened.

At first there was just a confusion of impressions. But then the one thing which refused to be moved from her consciousness by anything else was the absolute conviction that Erna Spolianska was better than herself.

Quentin Bannister might say what he liked. He would in any case! Marc might allow himself to be swayed by the thought that he had already told Gail the part was hers. But she knew – and she was almost certain that Oscar Warrender knew too – that the Polish girl could do something for Marc's opera which she, Gail, could not possibly do.

'It's not a question of work or coaching or even sheer devotion to the role,' Gail told herself. 'She *knows* what it's like to be the eternal exile. And I don't. Out of her misery and her experience she knows. Out of my good fortune and security I can only pretend. She deserves the part.

'But it's not only that. *Marc* deserves to have the very best person for the role. He has written a great role, a role that should go down in musical history. However good I may be – and I am good up to a point – I can only be a splendid copy of the real thing. She *is* the real thing. And Warrender knows it as well as I do.'

She wished she could talk to the conductor about it. But he was the last person in the world to brook questions from the wrong quarter. He would just think she was trying to 'pump' him about the final result.

As for the Bannisters, they both considered the matter settled. She winced at the very thought of what Quentin Bannister would say if she suggested that she should waste all the work and effort he had put into training her. And Marc would not thank her either if she assumed a self-sacrificing halo and insisted that she knew what was good for him, better than he knew himself. Yet, if she just let things go on as they were—

'Good lord, I thought everyone along this corridor had gone!' It was the hard-working pianist who put his head in at that moment. 'Why are you hanging about in this godforsaken hole?'

'I was just going.' Gail sprang to her feet and reached for her coat. 'Has everyone else gone?'

'Everyone except me. And Warrender. He was sorting out his notes a couple of minutes ago. He may have gone too by now. Well, I'm off, and you'd better be off too. The cleaners will be coming any minute. Though what they do here in the name of cleaning I wouldn't know. The place always looks a mess.'

'I shan't be a minute,' Gail said as he went out. Then she called after him, 'Where is Mr. Warrender?'

'In the front of the house. Why?' called back the pianist.

But Gail chose not to reply, and a few seconds later she heard the stage door swing on its rusty hinges.

She flung on her coat and, with only a moment's hesitation, went through once more to the front of the house. And there was Oscar Warrender standing by the orchestra rail, writing something on a sheaf of papers, his strong, handsome, rather forbidding face very clear-cut in the light from the one lamp near the piano.

'Mr. Warrender.' She stood a few feet away from him.

'Yes?' he said without looking up. 'Do you want to lock up?' He evidently mistook her for one of the theatre staff.

'No. I want to speak to you.' She caught her breath on a frightened little gasp, and he did look up then and recognize her.

'What is it?' He didn't sound specially pleased to see her. 'There's nothing more to say about the audition, if that's what you want. I told you – we shall be writing to you.'

Suddenly, what she must do was crystal clear to her, and she said, with hardly a tremor in her voice, 'I just wanted to say that I suppose – like me – you are well aware that Erna Spolianska is much better than I am.'

If she thought to startle him into a reply she was mistaken. Oscar Warrender was too old a hand for that. He glanced down at his papers and made a brief note – a trick he had when he wanted to disconcert anyone, as Anthea could have told her.

'Miss Rostall, are you asking for my personal opinion?'

'Yes, I am.'

'Well, naturally, I'm not going to give it to you. Why should I? In due course you will be told the final decision of the auditioning committee. To try to jump the gun with any individual member beforehand is highly irregular. But as you're young and inexperienced I won't hold that against you. Now run along.'

'No,' said Gail. 'I ha-haven't finished.'

Few people ever ventured to say 'No', when Oscar Warrender issued an order, and he gave a grim little smile, as though he found the experience novel – which he did.

'Then finish what you have to say quickly. You're being rather a nuisance, and I don't usually allow that.'

'Mr. Warrender, that girl knows more about the way Anya should be done than I shall ever know. She has a voice at least as good as mine. She doesn't use it quite so well—'

'No, she doesn't,' Warrender interjected, but Gail went on.

'That hardly matters, though. Her whole presentation of the part is stunning. Almost literally. It – it hits one, so that one can't think of anything but what she is singing. The work will be far more of a success with her than with me. Oh, I know both the Bannisters have voted for me—'

'*How* do you know?' inquired the conductor drily.

'It doesn't matter. As a matter of fact, Quentin Bannister backed me all along. He even coached me personally for the part.' That did make Warrender look up. she realized with some satisfaction. 'His pride in his own infallibility is mixed up with my getting the part. As for Marc—' her tone softened instinctively, though she was not aware of it – 'he made the friendly mistake of telling me some days ago that the part was mine. We even drank a champagne toast to my success,' she added wistfully. 'He feels he will be letting me down terribly now if I don't get the part.'

'He had no right to say any such thing,' said the conductor impatiently.

'No, of course he hadn't. But people are *human*, and make mistakes. At least some people do,' she muttered resentfully.

'I also make a few mistakes – if I take your point correctly,' Oscar Warrender told her sardonically. 'But not that kind of juvenile mistake. Well, what do you expect me to do about all this?'

'N-nothing. I just want you to know—' she took a deep breath and swallowed hard – 'I just want to tell you that I'm withdrawing from the contest. I don't intend to accept the role of Anya, even if it's offered to me.'

'No? Well, I think I must tell you, in return, Miss Rostall, that successful careers are not usually based on altruistic gestures to one's rivals. Is Miss Spolianska a friend of yours?'

'No.' Gail looked surprised. 'I've never spoken to her.'

'Then why—'

'Oh, it's not for *her*! At least, not primarily so. It's Marc I'm thinking of. I want his opera to be the most tremendous success.' And suddenly she smiled, as though she were already visualizing that success.

'I see,' said the conductor, and rubbed his chin meditatively. 'Is that the explanation you are going to give to other people? It won't go down well with Quentin Bannister, I assure you.'

'No explanation will go down well with him,' replied Gail resignedly. 'He'll be furious. But if I absolutely refuse to go on with it there's not much they can do about it, is there? And Erna Spolianska will undoubtedly get the part, won't she?'

'Undoubtedly. And what will you get? Apart from the satisfaction of knowing that you have served Marc's interests very generously.'

'I hadn't thought about that,' Gail admitted candidly.

'That doesn't seem very fair, does it?' The great conductor smiled at her suddenly. 'Besides, I think you would be in a stronger position if you could put forward the argument that you had been offered something else which appealed more to you.'

'But I haven't,' said Gail practically.

'One can always arrange these things.' Oscar Warrender spoke with the easy authority of someone who was used to pulling the strings in his own particular world. 'Once you have made – and announced – your decision, you had better be out of London. You are a first-class oratorio singer, Elsa Marburger tells me.'

'I'm rather good – yes,' Gail admitted.

'Never under-estimate yourself. It's just as affected and silly as showing off,' the conductor told her brusquely. 'I will send you to my friend Paul Winter in Hamburg. He is one of the few reliable agents, and has just been let down by the contralto he usually supplies for quite a number of secondary engagements throughout North Germany. It will be good, sound experience for you. You won't be singing with the top orchestras, but none of them will be bad.'

'Mr. Warrender, I – I can't thank you enough—'

'Don't thank me,' was the curt reply. 'You'll probably hate my guts when you're singing "Gerontius" in a small German town and you read of Spolianska's success in "The Exile".'

She did wince then. And he said, 'You're quite sure you want to do this?'

'Quite sure,' she insisted.

'Well, you're a good girl.' He suddenly held out his hand to her. 'If it's any joy to you, you have probably made the most handsome contribution to Marc Bannister's career that anyone is ever likely to make.'

'Do you *mean* that?' She stared at him wide-eyed.

'Yes, I do. In my view Marc Bannister has written a very fine opera, possibly a great one. But it needs careful casting. I would have been prepared – reluctantly prepared – to accept you in the part of Anya, because everything you do is musical and tasteful. But when I heard the Spolianska girl I knew she was a gift from heaven. Marc would be a fool to turn her down in any circumstances, and I can't think he doesn't know it in his heart. If I'd written a work like "The Exile" and was offered Spolianska, I'd have done murder, I think, to secure her.'

'But then Marc isn't ruthless, is he? And you are, where your art is concerned.'

'So they tell me,' replied Warrender indifferently. 'Now we must decide how we're going to handle this. How frank are we going to be with Marc himself?'

'We can't be frank at all,' cried Gail in great alarm. 'He'd be furious – and perhaps reject the whole idea – if he knew you and I were concocting something we thought was for his good. He's almost pathological about being allowed to make his own decisions in his own way. You see, his father—'

'We won't go into any father complexes,' interrupted the conductor, holding up his hand. 'Nothing is more boring. I think you must let us offer you the role. Probably the Bannisters have pretty well got a letter in the post already. You reply, saying you are honoured – or whatever term you like to use – but that you must reluctantly decline as you have unexpectedly been offered something you prefer—'

'Oh, Marc is going to hate that!' Suddenly she put up her hands to her cheeks.

'No one is going to like any of it much,' replied Warrender impatiently. 'But then we're not out to please people. We're out to save Marc's opera – and, incidentally, Marc himself from his own romantic foolishness in handing you the part before he had any right to do so.'

'Yes,' agreed Gail humbly.

'He'll be relieved, really. And while he's trying to conceal his relief, and his father is airing his disappointed fury, I shall say frankly that we are well out of a tricky situation and that in my view Spolianska will *make* the work.'

'Yes,' said Gail again, though she bit a trembling lip. 'That seems the best way.'

'Meanwhile,' went on the conductor not unkindly, 'I shall telephone to Hamburg tonight, and you will be hearing from Paul Winter within a day or two. Agreed?'

'Agreed,' Gail said rather forlornly.

'Then go along now.'

She turned away, but almost immediately he said, 'Miss Rostall' – and she turned back. 'Good luck. You deserve it.'

'Oh, thank you,' said Gail. And she went out of the theatre feeling just a little less wretched than she might have done.

The next few days, however, were the most difficult she had ever spent.

The letter offering her the role of Anya arrived the very next day. And she spent a couple of feverish hours concocting her refusal. Short of stating the real truth, and having both the Bannisters challenge her on every point, she could find no way of putting her refusal which was not either weak or offensive or both.

In the end, she made her letter brief and businesslike. But it seemed to her that her regrets, though politely expressed, rang hollow. And, once she had posted the letter, she lived in a state of near-panic lest either of the Bannisters should telephone or even call.

When the telephone did finally ring, two or three evenings later, she hardly dared to lift the receiver. But she need not have worried. It was Paul Winter, telephoning from Hamburg to ask if she could come across to be auditioned at the end of the following week. On the strength of Mr. Warrender's recommendation, he had several things in mind for her but must, naturally, hear her for himself.

Recklessly deciding to spend her small savings on the trip, Gail eagerly agreed. It was, of course, just the kind of chance that any aspiring singer would welcome, and at any other time she would have been ecstatic at the thought of going to sing for one of the leading German agents, on the recommendation of Oscar Warrender.

Indeed, for some hours her spirits rose to cheering heights. But then she thought of 'The Exile' and all she had thrown away, and she was immediately plunged into the depths again, as she wondered distractedly if she had really made a terrible mistake.

After all, she *was* good in the part. If Erna Spolianska had not turned up they would all – Warrender included – have moved heaven and earth to create a great performance, with Gail as the pivot. Could anyone say with certainty that they would not have succeeded? That was probably the way Marc had argued. And he had said he wanted her. He had *said* so.

But then she remembered Marc watching the Polish

girl as she sang her way through her big scene, and she knew she had been right to make this sacrifice. Not that Gail thought of it as a grand sacrifice. She thought of it as the only thing to do in the circumstances. Only she did wish she could have done it with Marc's friendly approval.

It was then that he telephoned. And the strange thing was that, though she had feared his call for days, when it came, for some reason or other, she thought it was Paul Winter once more from Hamburg. So her 'Yes?' was extremely eager. And her 'O-h—' when she realized who it was sounded chill with dismay.

'I – I can't argue about it, Marc,' she said quickly. 'I feel terribly badly. But I'm sure I am doing the right thing. And I know Erna Spolianska will do the part beautifully.'

'Thank you for the reassurance,' retorted Marc coldly, 'but I happened to want you in the part. However, as you say, there is no point in arguing about it now. All I want to know is – *what* is this dazzling offer that you prefer to the part of Anya?'

Momentarily she blessed Warrender for providing her with a real excuse.

'It – it's an offer from Germany. The kind of thing I never even hoped for. It will mean quite a lot of engagements in different towns. The experience will be invaluable. Mostly oratorio – which is really my line, of course. Different orchestras and different conductors—' She stopped suddenly, realizing she had been running on with feverish rapidity.

And Marc's voice said quietly, 'Who is arranging all this for you, Gail?'

'Paul Winter, of Hamburg,' she told him, with even a touch of innocent pride. For it *was* a pretty good offer, when all was said and done.

'Paul Winter? – of Hamburg?' He sounded incredulous for a moment. 'You don't say!' Then he gave a bitter little laugh and rather deliberately replaced the receiver.

At first she thought they had been cut off. She stared at her own receiver for a moment. Then she replaced it and waited.

But nothing happened. She even thought of phoning him back. But she had no idea where he was. And anyway she had the distinct and dreadful impression that he had no wish to speak to her again – ever.

The next day, at her lesson, she told Madame Marburger as much of the story as she felt she could. With her, of course, she had to be considerably more frank than with Marc.

'I refused the role,' she stated almost defiantly. 'I just couldn't take it after hearing and seeing what that girl could do with it. It wouldn't have been fair to anyone. Not to her, or Marc – or even to myself, I suppose.'

'But you were offered the role, Gail?'

'Oh, yes. Partly because there was a lot of pressure from Mr. Bannister, I imagine. But Oscar Warrender wanted Spolianska.'

'How do you know?' Her teacher glanced at her quickly.

'I had a word with him alone. The chance offered, and I took it. He didn't want to commit himself at first, of course, but in the end he admitted it. He thought I was right to refuse. And – and he arranged for me to have something else instead.'

'Something else instead?' Madame Marburger looked astonished. 'As a bribe, do you mean?'

'Oh, no! As a sort of reward, I suppose.' She laughed slightly but without much real amusement. Then she explained about the offer from Paul Winter, and immediately her teacher's whole manner changed.

'Well, Gail, I can't say anything but that I'm glad,' Madame Marburger stated emphatically. 'It will give you just the sort of experience you need at this juncture. Whereas, good as you were in Marc Bannister's opera, I am bound to admit the other girl was much better. You must forgive my frankness. A good teacher, like a good friend, should sometimes be impersonally candid.'

'I don't mind a bit,' Gail assured her. 'In fact, I'm rather relieved, I suppose, to have you confirm my own view. It makes me feel less as though I may have thrown away the chance of a lifetime.'

'There will be other chances,' her teacher assured her with a smile. 'You are too good for there not to be.' And Gail left the studio feeling cheered.

She had hardly gone more than twenty steps, however, before someone caught her lightly by the arm, and Oliver's half amused, half reproachful voice said, '*You've* set the cat among the Bannister pigeons, haven't you?'

'Oh, Oliver—' she was relieved at the friendly greeting, though alarmed at the thought of what he might have to tell her. 'Was there an awful to-do after I refused the part?'

'Frightful,' Oliver assured her cheerfully. 'Father was in such a rage that he even let slip the fact that he'd spent hours of work coaching you himself. And that didn't go down well with Marc, I can tell you.'

'I never meant Marc to *know* that,' she exclaimed in great dismay.

'Well, he knows now, and your copybook is well and truly blotted. Forget about it, love! There are some things one never can explain away, and this is one of them. Don't worry about it. Just write it off. There's nothing

148

else to do. What *I* really want to know is – what on earth was this glorious alternative which made even the leading role in Marc's new opera seem small beer?'

'Don't exaggerate,' said Gail nervously. 'It's not so glorious as all that. It just happens to be the very thing I need at my present stage of development.' She was grateful to Madame Marburger for having pointed that out to her. 'Paul Winter, the big Hamburg agent, is arranging a series of appearances for me in North Germany, and—'

'Paul Winter,' repeated Oliver, and he whistled. But in protest rather than admiration, she thought, and she asked sharply,

'Why not?'

'Don't you really know?'

Gail shook her head.

'Why, it was Paul Winter who gave such a boost to Lena Dorman's career just after *she'd* given Marc the brush-off. It's not the nicest way of making history repeat itself, is it?'

CHAPTER EIGHT

OLIVER was quite right, of course. There were some things one could never explain away. And to Gail it seemed that, even if she could bring herself to try to explain to Marc (an inconceivable thought, in any case) there was absolutely nothing she could say which would make him think her conduct anything but deplorable. She had, however unwittingly, hurt and humiliated him beyond bearing. And when she thought of that she could have buried her face in her hands and wept.

Indeed, when she got home after that revealing talk with Oliver, that was exactly what she did. She tried to put into practice his excellent advice that she had better just write off the whole affair and try to forget it. But each time she recalled that happy, happy evening when she and Marc had drunk champagne and toasted her future success, she knew *that* was something she would never forget. Even if she had to think of it now as a sort of lost glimpse of paradise.

She heard no more from Oscar Warrender. Having pulled the strings for her in an Olympian sort of way, he left the rest to her. And rightly so, of course.

Of Quentin Bannister she also heard nothing, which did not surprise her. She supposed there was something to be said for his being furious with her. Seldom could he have bestirred himself to give so much care and thought to any student's development. And, if his motives had not been unmixed, the fact remained that she had benefited by his training to an incalculable degree. There were some things he had taught her in the course of coaching her for the role of Anya which would stand her in good stead for the rest of her life.

If the situation had been less complicated she would have liked to tell him how much she truly appreciated what he had done for her, and how genuinely sorry she was that she had not been able to fulfil his hopes for her. But there was no way of contacting him now. And she could not imagine that it would give him any pleasure if she did.

Without the prospect of her journey to Hamburg to be auditioned by Paul Winter, life would have been sad indeed. But the exciting challenge of an entirely new phase in her career could not leave her unmoved, and there were moments when she felt her spirits rise irrepressibly. She even allowed herself to hope that some day, some time, she might unexpectedly meet Marc again and tell him something of the truth.

Not next month, of course. Not even perhaps next year. Too much was still involved. But one (unspecified) glorious day, when they would meet without bitterness and she could explain to him that she had longed to sing Anya but knew – as he himself would have discovered by then – that Erna Spolianska could do for his work what she could never do. Then she could explain about Oscar Warrender's offer, and he would see that she had been quite innocent of any desire to hurt or humiliate him.

It was all rather vague and improbable, of course. But she went over the whole scene in her own mind during the journey to Hamburg, and it consoled her quite considerably. It also steadied her nerves for the ordeal ahead.

In point of fact, owing to the warm recommendation from Warrender, she received from Paul Winter much less cavalier treatment than the busy agent usually meted out to new aspiring artists. Besides, he really was in a dilemma, having been let down by one of his principal artists, and he badly needed someone as gifted and well trained as Gail.

He paid her several compliments – which was unusual with him, had she but known it – and it seemed he would have no difficulty in arranging a three months' tour for her, beginning in the New Year.

Gail, who was full of good resolutions not to be anywhere near London while the preparations for the production of 'The Exile' were in progress, was somewhat dismayed at the prospect of returning to England within a matter of days. She had almost convinced herself that her engagements would follow practically immediately on the audition, provided she was found suitable. But the agent quickly disabused her of any such notion.

'Nothing is arranged as quickly as that, even in a moderate emergency,' he told her. 'You can stay here and practise your German and work on your singing, of course. I can recommend you to a modest *pension* and a good teacher. But, from the practical point of view, you will not be earning money until January.'

'Then I'll go home and spend Christmas with my family,' Gail said, realizing that this would be as happy a way as any of being out of London until she finally left for Germany.

'Very good. Christmas is a time to be with one's family,' agreed the agent, who was almost totally indifferent to his own family. But, like most Germans, he was sentimental in thought if not in deed, and the two words 'Christmas' and 'family' clicked together suitably in his mind.

So, to the delight of her parents and the twins, Gail

spent Christmas in the north, at home.

They were tremendously impressed to learn that she was actually to have a modest tour abroad, and her brother and sister at any rate talked as though she were already a star of the first magnitude.

'It's only a beginning,' Gail explained hastily. 'Quite good money and marvellous experience – with a chance to make useful contacts. But nothing absolutely sensational.'

'How did it come about, dear?' her mother inquired, with almost equal interest. 'Did you contact this Mr. Winter yourself on the chance of his having something? or did you have a recommendation to him – or what?'

'I had a recommendation. From Oscar Warrender.' She could not keep a slight note of pride out of her voice, and everyone was suitably awed. Especially her mother's next-door neighbour, Mrs. Panton, who was considered locally to be something of an authority on matters musical, and had dropped in to hear the latest from London in whatever form Gail chose to put it.

'Oscar Warrender?' she exclaimed. 'Why, he's among the very greatest conductors in the world. How *did* you get a recommendation from him, Gail?'

'He heard me at an audition,' Gail explained as casually as she could. 'I was short-listed for the leading role in a new opera and—'

'*Not* "The Exile"?' said Mrs. Panton, who read her musical periodicals with great thoroughness.

'Yes.' Gail was slightly taken aback to find herself involved in discussing the very thing she had most wished to avoid.

'Why, even I have heard of that,' declared her young sister, Veronica. 'Everyone's heard of it. Why didn't you get the part?' It was touchingly obvious that she could not imagine anyone rejecting her sister, once Gail had been heard.

'Someone else was much better.' Gail laughed lightly, though suddenly she was aware of almost unbearable heartache.

'I don't believe it,' stated Veronica with loyal incredulity.

'True, nevertheless, Vonnie.' Gail smiled at her. 'She was a Polish girl. I was there myself when she was auditioned. She was simply marvellous. With a deep understanding of the part which few people could achieve, I'm sure.'

'Were you terribly disappointed?' Veronica's eyes were wide with sympathy.

'Well, yes. It's no good pretending that I wasn't.' All at once she seemed to be back in that shabby theatre, watching Erna Spolianska's incredible performance – and then Marc's fascinated expression. 'I knew I was very near getting the part, and I'd even hoped it was virtually mine, because I'd had one or two hints that I was well in the running. But when I heard this girl I knew she was right for the part, and because I wanted the work to be a great success, I suppose I could just bear being pipped at the post.'

She managed to laugh a little as she said that, and the lighthearted expression helped to make her statement less than tragic.

'All the same, I think you're being wonderfully philosophical,' her mother remarked.

'Though of course it was quite gratifying to get even as near as that,' said Mrs. Panton.

'Well, I think it was a shame,' exclaimed Veronica. 'I think you should have had the part. Didn't you nearly burst into tears on the spot, Gail?'

'No,' said Gail, and smiled again.

But she thought to herself – the tears came later. And not so much for the disappointment about losing the part as for the anguish of knowing she had lost Marc's good opinion and friendship.

She had time to think much more deeply about her own reactions during the relaxed days at home, and she was both dismayed and surprised to find how precious those few happy hours with Marc had become in retrospect. Even at the time, of course, she had known that she was tremendously happy. That afternoon when he had bought her the china figure, that celebration supper together, the concert, the occasional word or glance which expressed so much with such unexpected warmth. Even, when she thought about it now, that sharp encounter at his own home, that very first evening.

Nothing of their all too brief relationship lacked its significance now. Not even her now confused thoughts at the time. When she had stood in front of the mirror, for instance, and laughingly asked herself if she wanted him to love her a little. And the instantaneous reply that she wanted him to love her a lot.

'It was a silly dream,' she told herself with a sigh. 'It was lovely – lovely, while it lasted. But it was just a dream.'

Only sometimes it seemed to be a dream from which it was impossible to wake up.

While she was still at home a long and rather fulsome article about the Bannister brothers appeared in one of the chattier newspapers. And just as Gail was completing her packing for her German trip, Veronica came rushing into her room with the paper in her hand.

'There's quite a lot here about Marc Bannister and "The Exile",' she announced. 'And quite a bit about the other brother too. Shall I read it to you?'

'Yes, read it to me,' said Gail with an indulgent smile. And although she had to repress a slight quiver of nervous apprehension, she went on folding dresses with a calm and competent air.

The article dealt pretty accurately with Marc's career to date, and then went into some detail about the forthcoming production of 'The Exile'. There was a little about all the principal members of the cast, with a reference to the fact that the leading woman's role was to be sung by Erna Spolianska.

Veronica stumbled slightly over the name and then said, 'They describe her as unknown in this country, but coming from abroad with a fine reputation. And they say Oscar Warrender is going to conduct the first performance, which will be towards the end of March— Oh, I say! you'll still be in Germany, won't you? Will you be sorry – or glad?'

'I don't really know,' Gail confessed frankly.

'Mostly glad, I should think,' said her sister. 'I should think it would be agony watching someone else do a part that you'd hoped to do yourself.'

'Not if she does it as marvellously, as I think she will. But, all things considered—' by which she supposed she meant both Marc and Quentin Bannister – 'I expect it would be better for me not to be there. Perhaps it's just as well that I shall be in Germany. But you'll have to look out for the reviews, Vonnie, and send them all to me. You will, won't you?'

'You bet!' Veronica was pleased and proud to have even so modest a hand in things. 'There's nothing more in the article about Marc Bannister. But they say the other brother is also engaged in musical composition of a different sort. That's how they put it. His name's Oliver.

Do you know him too?'

'Yes. Very well. It was he who first took me down to the Bannister home.'

'You know everyone, don't you?' said Veronica admiringly.

'Not exactly. Read me what they say about Oliver.'

'He's been writing the music for a new revue. And according to this article he's just as brilliant as his brother, only in a different way. The book of the revue is by a man called Tom Mallender, and it's being put on at The Paragon in April, by J. R. Arrowmead. Do you know him too?'

'No, I can't say I do,' Gail laughed. 'But I know Tom Mallender. And the day he had lunch with Mr. Arrowmead and the idea was first mooted, I met him and he was so excited that he hardly knew where he was going or what he was doing. I'm so terribly glad it's all turned out well for them. They're both tremendously gifted men.'

'There are photographs here of both the Bannister brothers,' Veronica said. 'Do you want to see them?'

'Yes, please.' Gail held out her hand, and hoped that only she was aware that it was not quite steady.

Veronica handed over the newspaper and Gail stared, fascinated, at the very good photograph of Marc, looking rather serious, it was true, but so exactly as she had seen him look a dozen times that she could hardly bite back an exclamation of mingled pain and pleasure.

'Oliver's the better-looking one, isn't he?' observed her sister, glancing again at the photographs.

'Not really.' Gail looked passingly at the smiling picture of Oliver, and then back at Marc. And she was silent for such a long time that presently Veronica said doubtfully, 'Gail—?'

'Um–hm?'

'Are you in love with one of them?'

'Good heavens, no!' Gail dropped the paper. 'Of course not. Whatever gave you that idea?'

'The funny way you looked when you were examining those photographs. Only I couldn't quite make out which one you were really looking at. I think it's Marc you're rather keen on, though, isn't it?'

'Neither or them means anything special to me,' declared Gail, wondering how she could tell such a thumping lie without the ground opening and swallowing her. 'Oliver and I are really very good friends, in a gay, light-hearted sort of way. We were students together for quite a while. I never met Marc until Oliver took me down to their home in Sussex. He and his father were already looking round for the right cast for "The Exile" so my connection with him was almost entirely to do with professional matters.'

'Did *he* want you for the part of his heroine?'

'At first, I think he did.' She suddenly had a very clear picture of Marc smiling at her over the champagne glass. 'But not after he heard the Spolianska girl. I don't think anyone could *really* have preferred me then— And now I must get my packing finished, Vonnie. Leave the newspaper, if you don't want it, I'll take it with me and read the article myself at leisure.'

So Veronica left the newspaper where it was lying, and Gail presently slipped it into her case.

The next day she left for Germany.

Long afterwards, when she used to look back on those months in Germany, Gail found it difficult to decide if she had been happy or unhappy. Of course there was immense pleasure and interest in travelling through an entirely new country, with different experiences at every turn. But sometimes she was keenly aware that she had left at least half her heart at home in England.

She got on well with most of her colleagues. She was almost uniformly praised for her work. And she was aware that all the time she was enlarging her artistic horizons. All this could be counted as making for a very happy life. But whenever she was able to get hold of an English newspaper she scanned it eagerly for news of Marc and his opera – almost always without any result. Inevitably so. For while it was in process of production 'The Exile' hardly rated more than a line or two among miscellaneous items of news. It was not until its first night that it would become headline news.

Some of Gail's engagements were in quite small towns, many of indescribable charm and picturesque appeal, and always there was an appreciative audience. Occasionally she took part in quite important concerts in one of the larger towns, and on these occasions she had the genuine thrill of singing under the directorship of really distinguished conductors. But most of the time her conductors were good, hardworking, run-of-the-mill people, who knew their scores inside out, but brought no special flame of genius to the performance.

All of it was good experience, however, and forced as she was to speak little but German most of the time, she improved her command of the language out of all knowledge.

Quite early in the tour she struck up a friendship with an American girl, Liz Enderby, a gifted soubrette with an excellent Mozart style. She, of course, had no place in Gail's world of oratorio, but they had rooms at the same *pension* and sometimes travelled together when Liz was singing at one of the smaller opera houses and Gail had a concert engagement nearby.

She was warm-hearted and gay and very good company, and did more than anyone else to keep Gail from feeling too homesick. It was from Liz that Gail heard, for the first time after many, many weeks, the name which was constantly in her mind but never on her lips.

They were sitting late over breakfast one morning, in the bright little breakfast-room of their *pension*, when Liz said without looking up from her paper, 'I see Marc Bannister has a new opera coming on in London. It's the first night tonight.'

'Tonight?' There was a ring of such poignant interest in Gail's voice that the other girl did look up then.

'Do you know him?'

'Yes. I nearly got a part in his opera. Oh, I wish I'd known it was tonight. I think – I think I might have sent him a telegram or something.'

'There's still time,' said the practical Liz. 'Why don't you?'

'Oh, well—' Gail could not imagine why she had made such a ridiculous suggestion – 'no, I don't think I will. It's silly, somehow. What's one telegram among all the others on an occasion like a first night?'

'You're right,' agreed Liz. 'Why don't you call him instead?'

'*Call him?*'

'Well, ring him up. Isn't that what you say?' Liz grinned. 'Do just that. Call him.'

'I couldn't think of such a thing,' exclaimed Gail, panic-stricken, though she was already thinking very hard about it in a dazed sort of way.

'Sure you could! Don't be so British and reserved,' said the American girl. 'A call's much better than a cable. As you say, he'll get dozens of those. From all his friends and quite a lot of his enemies, if I know the musical world. And the sweeter the message the deadlier the hopes of failure. Come on, Gail. A call from abroad, just as he's feeling deathly – which he probably is right now—'

'*Now*! Do you mean – phone him now?' Gail was white except for a bright spot of colour in each cheek.

'Now's as good a time as any. Better than most. What are you scared about? It's only a short overseas call. I guess you can even dial it from here. If you're in such a state about a little call like this, what would you do if you were calling Texas, which is what I have to do whenever I want to speak to *my* heart-throb?'

Gail felt she should explain that Marc was not her heart-throb. But she was so unnerved by the whole conversation, after being weeks without the possibility of even uttering his name, that she remained silent.

'Do you know his number?' inquired the determined Liz.

'Yes. He'll be at his London flat, I expect.' Gail passed the tip of her tongue over her dry lips.

'Then it's simple. You don't even have to call "Information".'

'But what will he *think*?'

'He'll think, "Fancy that angel child calling me all the way from Germany. Things *have* to be all right now." And he'll be just crazy over the idea and not feel so badly about tonight.'

Gail could not imagine Marc in any circumstances thinking of her in those strange terms. But the idea that she might have a reason – *any* reason – for speaking to him, if only for two minutes made her feel slightly intoxicated.

That was the only reason that she could give to herself afterwards for what she did. That and the fact that the impulsive Liz – who always preferred action to discussion – refused to listen to any excuses.

'Go on, you silly! If you know him, call him. If you don't know him, admit as much, and we'll drop the subject.'

Somehow it was that which stung Gail into final capitulation. That the overwhelming reality of her life should be shadowed by doubts was simply not to be borne. She went into the little telephone room and dialled Marc's number. And before she could drop the receiver, in terror at what she was doing, his voice replied. So clearly that he might have been standing at her elbow.

'Yes? Marc Bannister speaking.'

'Oh, Marc!' She thought she heard him catch his breath, so he must have recognized her voice immediately. 'Please don't be angry with me for phoning—' that was not quite what she had meant to say, but it slipped out involuntarily—'I just *had* to wish you luck for tonight.'

There was a slight pause. Then he said, rather formally, 'That's very kind of you, Gail. Where are you calling from?'

'Hamburg.'

'From Hamburg! You rang from Hamburg just to wish me luck? Oh, Gail—'

'It's awful being so far away just when everything is happening.' Suddenly she had found the right words. 'But my heart will be with you all in the Opera House tonight. Please tell Erna Spolianska that the girl who didn't get the part wishes her all the luck in the world.'

'I'll tell her. She'll be truly touched. She's a generous-hearted girl herself—'

'Is she wonderful in the part, Marc?'

'Yes, she's wonderful,' he said. And then, before she could ask him to enlarge on that – 'How are things with you, Gail?'

'Fine, thank you. I'm getting a lot of useful experience.'

'And are you happy?'

'Happy?' she repeated the word, a little as though she hardly knew its meaning. 'Why do you ask that, Marc?'

And then the line went dead. And she could not decide if she had been cut off, or if he thought the conversation had gone far enough. She tried to find out from an indifferent operator, but all she could get was that it was impossible to reconnect her as the line was temporarily overloaded.

She hardly thought she would have asked to be reconnected, anyway. If Marc had said all he wished to say, he would hardly welcome a second call. She had had her moment. Much, much more than anything she could have dreamed of even an hour ago. She must be satisfied.

For most of the day she *was* satisfied. During the long afternoon journey out to the small town where she was singing that night she pretended to be asleep, so that her colleagues should not try to engage her in conversation. But behind her closed eyelids she was visualizing, with the utmost clarity, what was happening in London. In turn, she imagined how Marc, how Quentin Bannister, how Spolianska, how Oscar Warrender – and again how Marc – would be passing the long afternoon hours until the evening that was to put all their hopes to the test.

And if she had not deliberately thrown away her chance, she too could have been part of that great occasion. She too would have been one of the central characters. If she had not acted so impulsively— If Oscar Warrender had not sealed her decision by the offer to send her to Germany—

It was then that she suddenly remembered the great conductor saying sardonically, 'Don't thank me. You'll probably hate my guts when you're singing in a small German town and you read of Spolianska's success in "The Exile".'

Well, she didn't hate him. The decision had been hers, and hers alone. But she did wonder, for a dreadful few minutes, why ever she had made it.

She got through the evening's performance somehow. She got through the long, late journey back to Hamburg. She fell into bed so exhausted that at least she slept immediately. And she woke to the knowledge that she must still wait some hours before the newspapers from England arrived.

Even then possibly the criticisms would have been held over until the next day in the continental editions.

They were. But spread across two columns of the front page, as a major news item, ran the headline, 'Cheers for Great New British Opera'.

She read every word of the enthusiastic, if rather superficial, report. And when the full musical criticisms came later she read every word of them too. Finally, when Veronica – faithful to her promise – sent every newspaper cutting she could put her hand upon, including the Sunday papers, she devoured them and then sat back and said aloud,

'It's true. There's hardly a sour note in the whole lot. Marc has become in a night a famous composer.'

But the criticism which gave her the deepest satisfaction of all was the one which said, 'In any circumstances "The Exile" would be rated a fine opera. With Erna Spolianska in the role of Anya, it becomes a great human work.'

She had been right to stand down.

During her last two weeks in Germany Gail was almost completely happy. All her anxious doubts about her decision had been resolved, and now she could hardly wait to see the performance for herself. She would slip in one evening unobserved and just hear and see for herself what Marc's work was like, given perfect casting.

In addition, she knew that she had given a good account of herself during her modest tour in Germany, and it seemed certain that she would be asked back again at no distant date. Her own career, then, had not received any serious setback from what she had done. Rather the reverse. And, finally, that brief telephone conversation with Marc did rouse in her the hope that they were still friends to a very small degree.

Indeed, on the way back to England, she even indulged in some day-dreams in which Marc sought her out for the express purpose of finishing that interrupted conversation. But, as her imagination would not take her any further than that, she had to leave the dream unfinished too.

The sight of the familiar street, as the taxi drove up to her front door, almost brought a lump into her throat, and she realized that she must have been a good deal more homesick than she knew during the three months she had been away. And as she climbed the stairs even her luggage could not weigh down the lightness of her heart.

At the very moment when she opened the door of her flat the telephone began to ring. And so appropriate did this seem to her dream about Marc that she rushed to pick up the receiver, not supposing for one moment that it could be anyone but him.

It was Oliver's voice which spoke, however, in tones of the greatest urgency.

'Gail! Thank heaven you're at home!'

'At home? I've only just this moment put my foot inside the door after three months away. I haven't even taken my coat off.'

'Then don't,' was the curt reply. 'Come round here at once. Tom and I need you as we've never needed anyone in our lives before. Hop into a taxi and come round to Tom's studio.'

'But what's the matter?' Gail cried. 'What's happened?'

'Jane Purdie – the girl who's been rehearsed for all the songs that were *your* songs – has had an accident and broken her leg. The opening night is next Tuesday. We've only five days to go, and you're the only one who can save the show for us. You know the "feel" of those numbers as well as we know it ourselves. You can't refuse us this time, Gail. You can't!'

'No – I can't refuse this time,' Gail agreed slowly. 'All right, Oliver, I'll come.'

And without so much as a glance round her dusty little flat, Gail caught up her handbag and gloves and went out, closing the front door behind her.

CHAPTER NINE

WHEN Gail arrived at Tom Mallender's studio, she found Oliver walking up and down restlessly while Tom, lying full length in an armchair, his legs thrust out in front of him, looked the picture of silent gloom.

'Here she is!' exclaimed Oliver as Gail walked in, having been admitted by the cleaning woman who looked after Tom, and who had greeted her with a gusty whisper of, 'They're all of a heap, poor young gentlemen – both of them.'

'When did it happen?' Gail took off her coat and flung it on a chair, without even referring to the three months' gap since they had seen each other.

'Two hours ago. We'd just heard when I phoned you,' said Oliver. 'It was all I could think of doing,' he added rather pathetically, Gail thought. And it seemed to her that they were both as helpless as her own young brother and sister would have been in like circumstances.

'Well, that was very sensible of you,' she told him bracingly. 'We've got five days, you say? We can do it all right in five days. Get up, Tom, and stop looking like a lost soul. It isn't the end of—'

'I *am* a lost soul,' replied Tom dramatically. 'This was the chance of a lifetime, and now the whole thing is doomed to failure. The luck's run out. Jane was half the show. Well, a third of it, anyway. It can't be anything but the most hopeless flop now.'

'Don't be such a drip!'

She gave him a smart little kick on the ankle, which made him draw in his long legs and sit up quickly and say,

'Here! That *hurt*!'

'It was meant to hurt,' Gail assured him callously. 'It was meant to recall you to realities and stop you from wallowing in cowardly self-pity. It's true you've lost Jane What's-her-name, and I'm terribly sorry for her and you. But you've got me instead. And only three months ago you were ready to beat a pathway to my front door with your pleas for me to join you. Come on and show me what I have to do. I bet Jane was no better in that Spanish number than I was.'

'She's right, you know.' Oliver stopped walking up and down the room and looked a trifle brighter. 'We said from the beginning that, good though Jane was, she wasn't a patch on Gail.'

'Since then Gail's been working her way round Europe on "Messiah" or something,' Tom said sourly. 'She'll have spoiled her revue style.' But he got to his feet and looked less suicidal.

'Conceal your ignorance, if you can,' Gail told him crisply. 'I didn't sing in "Messiah" as it happens. But a good Handel style fits one for any type of singing. And *he* knew what the public wanted, if anyone ever did. Why are we wasting time? And how many numbers did Jane have in the show?'

'Five. But two of them can go to another girl who was almost equally good.' Suddenly Tom seemed to come out from under his cloud of gloom and begin to make plans. 'They are on the edge of broad comedy, and she's a funny little cuss, which you are not. Oliver will have to transpose them for her, because she's a light soprano so far as she's anything. But that doesn't matter. She's dead funny, and her voice is quite a secondary matter.'

'Well, that leaves us with three numbers for me. What makes you think I can't manage that, you mutt? I take it the Spanish scene is one of them?'

'Yes, of course.' Tom regarded her with a touch of new respect and then said to Oliver, 'I say, she's changed a bit, hasn't she? Less of the dew and more of the vitriol. She'll be good in the Greek scene.'

'*Greek* scene?' Gail looked surprised and intrigued. 'That doesn't sound much like revue.'

'Oh, it's a sort of skit, of course, on the scene where Paris couldn't decide to which of the three goddesses to award the golden apple. It's rather funny, to tell the truth.'

'I'm sure it is,' Gail said encouragingly. 'Which of the three am I?'

'Hera. You have to have a dark voice for the Queen of Heaven when she's in a temper.'

'As Wagner discovered long ago,' murmured Gail.

But when Tom asked, 'What did you say?' she replied lightly, 'Oh, nothing. Let's get on.'

So for the next two hours they went over the three numbers in which Gail was to star, as Tom expressed it.

'Star?' said Gail doubtfully. 'Do three numbers make a star?'

'One number can do it — if it's the right number and the right artist. And the way you do these three — yes,' stated Tom, who was a mercurial creature and had now completely recovered his customary good spirits and enthusiasm. 'Lord, I'd forgotten how good you were! And you've got more assurance — more real professionalism — now. You take the stage, as it were, in a way you didn't before, good though you were in the studio sense of the term.'

'Well, I've had a good bit of professional experience since I first sang for you,' Gail reminded him with a smile.

'Only standing sedately on a platform singing oratorio,' countered Oliver, though not so disparagingly as Tom spoke of her usual work.

'I also had a lot of training from your father.' Gail looked straight at him. 'Remember?'

'Oh – yes, that too.' Oliver grinned reflectively. 'I don't think he's forgiven you yet, by the way. He must have worked harder on you than he ever did on anyone else, if he's to be believed.'

'He gave me the most wonderful concentrated coaching,' Gail said earnestly. 'I owe him more than I could possibly say. He taught me things about phrasing and colouring that I'll never forget. I was using some of that, though unconsciously perhaps, in these three numbers, believe it or not.'

'Nice work. And it's generous of you to talk like that.' Oliver patted her shoulder. 'You know, of course, that "The Exile" was an unqualified success?'

'Yes, I know.'

'In a way, I suppose even Marc knows now that it was a sort of stroke of good fortune that you preferred that other chance, in Germany. Spolianska was a knock-out in the part of Anya. I'll never forget how the house rose to her on that first night. And, good though I don't doubt you were in the part, she was something so special that I don't think anyone else could have approached her, if you don't mind my saying so.'

'No, Oliver, I don't mind a bit. In fact, I'm glad to hear you say so. I knew she could be the making of the work, even at that first audition. That helped me to take my decision. I mean—' she added hastily – 'it made me feel that I wasn't entirely letting Marc down by refusing the role.'

'You're not half as glad about it all as we are,' Tom put

in. 'I suppose if you'd made a thumping success in Marc's opera you could hardly have come to our rescue now. A few revue numbers would have been beneath your musical dignity and all that.'

'Which brings us to the point that it might be better for you to take another name for this occasion, Gail,' said Oliver quite seriously. 'It might not be a good thing for your real career to be associated with this, now you're making a success abroad and so on. Like people who write thrillers under one name and real egg-head books under another, you know.'

'Don't be an intellectual snob,' retorted Gail. 'Particularly about your own excellent work. Whatever I do I do under my own name. If I do it to the best of my ability *I'm* not ashamed of it. If it's worth doing, it's worth doing well and being acknowledged.'

'You know, I've always liked this girl.' Tom patted her on her smooth auburn head. 'And I feel by the pricking of my thumbs – which are very reliable thumbs in these matters – that she's going to be our lucky mascot.'

Gail refrained from asking what his thumbs had been doing two hours ago, when he was sure that neither she nor anyone else could rescue his show from disaster. Tom was, as he had himself said modestly on more than one occasion, something of a genius. And geniuses must be permitted a few inconsistencies.

That at least she had learned from the Bannisters!

The next few days were the most crowded and concentrated she had ever known. Indeed, it was sheer necessity as well as inclination which decided her not to contact anyone in her usual circle with the news that she was back in London. Better they should assume that she was still away.

Particularly did she feel this was the case with

Madame Marburger who might, for all she knew, strenuously object to her taking part in anything so far removed from her usual type of work. Not that Gail did not feel able to stand up to almost any kind of opposition nowadays. She had learned a great deal in the last few months. But if all friction *could* be avoided before the great first night, that was all to the good.

For the first time in her life she had the delightful experience of being fitted for highly glamorous stage clothes. Her Greek costume was enchanting, her Spanish one almost shockingly striking, but the really beautiful costume was the one for her third appearance.

This was to be in the central act of the evening. It was a short romantic drama set in seventeenth-century France, and Gail simply had to make an appearance as an opera singer of the period and sing a couple of Lully airs, which had considerable dramatic point in the play. It was necessary that her costume should be a real show-stopper, and this was the kind of thing that Reuben Arrowmead's stage designers could do to perfection.

Never had Gail supposed that she could look as she did when she surveyed herself in the long stage mirror just before the dress rehearsal. And Tom's uninhibited, 'Lord! You're really a beauty, Gail!' did wonderful things for her ego.

It was not until after the dress rehearsal – a pretty successful dress rehearsal, though a certain amount of hair-tearing went on – that Gail ventured to say to Oliver, 'Will your family be coming tomorrow night?'

'But of course! However condescending Father may permit himself to be, there's great family solidarity about anything like this. He says he thinks it's going to be a great success. I hope he means it! He has a splendid nose for the subtle perfume of success.'

'I think it is too, Oliver.' She smiled encouragingly at him. 'I can't tell you why I'm so sure. But it's going to be all right.'

'I hope so,' said Oliver again. 'I've given up being able to judge coolly. I'm just a disgusting mass of nerves. *You* look cool enough.' He sounded almost resentful. 'Aren't you at all scared?'

'Not sickeningly so,' Gail replied with great exactness. 'I have my shivery moments, of course, when I think of actually being on the stage, with the theatre full. But I love my three scenes so much that I can't believe other people won't love them too. – Is Marc coming?' she added casually.

'Oh, yes, I expect so.' Oliver spoke nervously and absently.

'Oliver, do they know I'm in it?'

'Do who know?' He looked past her and shouted an irritable direction to one of the stage hands.

'Your family,' she said patiently.

'What? – No, I haven't had time to talk to any of them in the last few days.'

'Then please don't tell them. I'd feel better somehow, if they didn't know beforehand. I know it probably isn't of any interest to any of them—' she paused, not allowing even to herself how eagerly she hoped Oliver would contradict her.

But his thoughts were obviously already on something else and he did not even bother to answer her. So she sighed a little and turned away. Perhaps it was just as well that no personal considerations should be allowed to colour those last few hours of concentrated thought about her work.

When she told Oliver that she was not overwhelmingly nervous it was nothing less than the truth. There *was* the occasional tremor, of course, on her own behalf, but most of her concern was for him and Tom. For them this revue was the first great test of their artistic collaboration. For her it was undoubtedly an important occasion. But it carried none of the all-consuming terror she would have experienced if she had had to sing Anya on the first night of 'The Exile', for instance.

This faint element of detachment – which she allowed herself only when she was not on the stage, of course – stood her in good stead when it came to that famous first night. She was calmer than almost anyone else backstage, and so she was one of the first to detect that indefinable current of delighted approval which began to flow almost immediately between audience and stage.

During her first scene, which was in the Greek skit, she could feel the warmth and good will of the audience coming over the footlights like a living force, and her sheer enjoyment of what she was doing imparted to her performance an unforced gaiety and charm which communicated itself to her colleagues and brought them the first undoubted ovation of the evening.

As she came off the stage she ran into Oliver, who was wandering up and down distractedly, chewing his shapely finger-nails like a frightened schoolboy.

'Don't, Oliver darling.' She gave him an affectionate hug. 'It's going marvellously. Can't you *hear* it is?'

'I know – I know. You were terrific.' He gave her a brief, absent-minded kiss. 'I just feel it simply can't go on like this.'

But it did. The evening was described afterwards, not unjustly, as a crescendo of success such as had not been seen and heard in the field of light entertainment for many a long day. Gaiety and mutual enjoyment coursed between audience and players, as though they were all in some delightful conspiracy together to have the time of their lives.

Much of it was sheer scintillating fun. But, mixed in, with a subtlety remarkable in two such young men, Tom and Oliver had provided several moments of real thought-provoking brilliance and touches of nostalgic heartache which added the occasional enjoyable tear to contrast with all the laughter.

Gail stopped the show all right with her entry in the seventeenth-century playlet, and her perfectly straight singing in the Lully arias brought her the kind of curtain that is every singer's dream.

But the real test of the evening for Gail was the Spanish number. Not only was the actual performance to be delicately balanced between laughter and tears. It was she herself who had suggested the particular way of doing it, and therefore she felt personally responsible for its success or failure.

Just before she went on to the stage she was, for the first time, suddenly and appallingly nervous. The idea of playing it for laughs to begin with and ending on a note of near-tragedy now seemed to her to be nothing but a gimmick. How terrible if the whole show sagged at this point because of her insistence that this was the way to do it!

She heard the familiar, utterly singable opening, and she was on stage almost before she knew what she was doing. Never in her life had she felt less comic. But she found something deep within her – in reality an instinctive vein of delicate comedy – which told her exactly how to play, and slightly overplay, her part.

There was not a breath of crudeness or coarseness, but she was unmistakably the girl who knew how to attract the men with everything in her figure, face and voice. She heard little ripples of appreciative laughter running through the house as she gave just the lilt and emphasis to the irresistible tune, which was to set everyone whistling or singing it the next morning.

Then, at the exact moment when amusement could have turned to uninhibited laughter, the complete change came. One man – obviously the one man who mattered to her – walked past with no more than a flicker of contemptuous rejection.

She stood there, quite still, just watching him go out of her life. And it was as though he stripped her of all her confidence and her charm, so that her very spirit seemed to droop.

And somehow, as she saw him vanish into the wings, Gail associated him in her own mind with the loss of Marc's friendship and affection; and she knew, as she had never known before, how to put into her voice the hunger and desolation for the ultimate loss of the one thing that really mattered.

With a little gesture of despairing resignation, she turned away and, half to herself – in a *mezzo voce* for which Elsa Marburger was certainly responsible! – she sang the catchy, provocative little tune again, and it became a lament for all shattered dreams.

She went slowly from the stage in utter silence. And then the applause came, like a tropical storm.

The song was itself a winner. Everyone knew that with instantaneous recognition. But it was Gail's presentation of it which sent it to the top pinnacle of success.

Nothing could fail after that, and the final numbers merely added a jewel or two to the diadem of success which already rested securely on the show. Gail remembered little of the rest until the congratulations and kisses and bouquets and applause which closed the performance.

Oliver and Tom Mallender had 'arrived'. And, beyond any shadow of doubt, Gail Rostall with them.

In all the excitement backstage, after the final fall of the curtain, Gail had little part to play. The two girls with whom she shared a dressing-room had their quota of friends and family to kiss and praise them, but Gail had no one. It was inevitable. For excellent reasons she had deliberately chosen not to tell anyone what she was doing. Even her family were to read of her success only in the next morning's newspapers.

She felt a trifle forlorn. Until Oliver looked in to thank and congratulate everyone and then drew her aside to whisper, 'Come to my room. The family want to see you.'

To Gail at that moment 'the family' meant above all Marc. And, although he managed to look calm as she accompanied Oliver, in reality her heart was thudding with mingled hope and dread. She had much to explain to him, and very little of it could be done on an occasion such as this. But surely, surely he would receive her kindly at last, and they could make some sort of bridge to a future meeting when full explanations could be made.

When they arrived at Oliver's room, however, though Quentin Bannister and his wife were conspicuous among the throng, there was no sign of Marc.

Her disappointment was so absolute that she felt strangely like the real-life version of the Spanish girl she had portrayed so successfully. But at least the intensity of her feeling helped her to face the confrontation with Quentin Bannister, if not with indifference, with a certain composure.

'Well, you naughty girl—' he surveyed her sternly. 'I suppose you're expecting to be forgiven after tonight's triumph?'

'I should like to think I might *hope* to be forgiven,' she replied, with becoming meekness.

'On the principle that, if you help one member of the family, you can afford to affront another one, I suppose?'

'Not – quite.' Gail felt sure he thought she ought to hang her head at this point, so she looked down fixedly at her shoes. 'I want to take this chance of saying that I do know how much I owe to you, and that what you taught me will stand me in good stead for the rest of my life. I'm sorry I just couldn't fulfil your hopes for me entirely, Mr. Bannister. But the fact is that, by standing down over Anya, I did leave the place free for the ideal person, from all accounts.'

'A lot you cared about *that* when you slapped Marc and me in the face, and went gallivanting off to Germany on your own.'

'Did – did Marc also feel that I slapped him in the face, as you put it?'

'Of course he did. And, family rivalries and stresses being what they are, I don't expect he's any better pleased now he finds you were willing to put yourself very much at the service of Oliver's career, though you wouldn't even play fair by him.'

'*Oh!*' Gail stopped contemplating her shoes and looked up in sudden horror. 'You don't mean that's how he thinks of it, do you?'

'Well, of course. How else should he view your behaviour? Well—' as Gail remained dumb with dismay – 'I suppose those of us who are big enough can take a good deal of ingratitude in our stride.' By which he evidently meant himself rather than Marc.

But, as he was turning away, Gail caught him by the

arm and exclaimed, 'Mr. Bannister—'

'All right, all right. You're forgiven,' he said magnanimously. But he very firmly removed the fingers which were clenched on his arm and proceeded to talk to someone else.

Gail was desolated. Quentin Bannister's good humour would extend to no further discussion, she could see, and her hands dropped helplessly to her sides. At the same moment, Mrs. Bannister, whose presence she had completely forgotten, said quietly beside her,

'Gail dear, this is the second time I have to thank you for a great service to my family.'

'Mrs. Bannister—' Gail turned in astonishment to receive the cool, sweet kiss which was deposited on her cheek. 'I don't think I – I know what you mean.'

'Don't you?' For a moment Gail had the full impact of the smile which had made Daisy Bannister famous thirty years ago. 'I know for you it's primarily your own evening of triumph. But you have also helped to set Oliver on a splendid career, if all the signs mean anything.'

'That – yes,' Gail smiled faintly in return. 'And I'm very glad it should be so. But, for the rest – Don't *you* think I let Marc down very shabbily, then?'

'Oh, no. Anya *had* to be played by Spolianska, didn't she? You knew that. And that was why you removed yourself from the scene.'

'Mrs. Bannister,' said Gail again, and rather helplessly this time, 'how did you know?'

'Because I am really quite a far-seeing and intelligent woman,' was the cool reply. 'Though it often pays me to appear otherwise.'

Gail gave a delighted little laugh. And then she said shyly, 'I'm glad you feel like that about me.'

'Gail dear, I want you to think hard.' Those very

beautiful eyes, which were singularly like Marc's when he was in a softer mood, contemplated Gail thoughtfully. 'If there is anything you want very much, and which I can do for you, you only have to ask.'

'If there's anything—' repeated Gail, and then she stopped. She was silent for almost half a minute. And then because, she knew suddenly that this was one of the great moments of truth in her life, she said slowly, 'Would you please ask me down to your home again some time?'

'Next Sunday,' replied Mrs. Bannister, with incredible exactness for a seemingly vague person. 'There is a good train from Victoria at eleven o'clock. I will meet you at the station at twelve-ten. You must stay overnight and go back on Monday in time for your evening perforamnce.'

'Oh, *thank* you!' Gail was not quite sure if she were terrified or enraptured at the speed with which this had been arranged. But as Quentin Bannister indicated at this moment that it was time he and his wife went, there was no chance to modify, or even discuss the arrangements.

As Mrs. Bannister bade her good-night, however, she said quietly, 'I shall see Marc is there.' And then they were both gone, and Gail was left wondering if it had all really happened.

She went out to a late supper with Oliver and Tom Mallender, and they shared in a daze of mutual relief, congratulation and wild optimism.

'We haven't seen the reviews yet,' Gail said warningly once.

But, 'We don't need to,' replied Tom. 'If they damned us unanimously – which is unlikely – they could only hold back the tide for a week or two.'

'By the way, was Marc there in the end?' Gail turned casually to Oliver.

'Of course. He thought you fine.'

'He didn't bother to come and say so.'

'No? – I remember now, he left before the parents. Maybe he's still a bit sore that you preferred revue to opera, so far as the Bannisters are concerned,' Oliver replied complacently.

And though Gail winced at the repeated expression of opinion, she found herself quite unable to challenge it.

The reviews the next morning were almost uniformly good, and Gail was singled out for special mention in all the principal ones. This naturally brought ecstatic and astonished telephone calls from the family, and necessitated explanations of great length and complexity.

Explaining to Madame Marburger was not quite so easy. But, once she had been persuaded to come and see the show for herself, she expressed a qualified degree of pleasure in her pupil's performance.

'It isn't what I would have chosen for you, Gail, and I can't pretend otherwise. But your performance is tasteful and musical to the highest degree. I admit that freely. So long as you don't become completely side-tracked, the experience may be of value.'

Which was the most, Gail felt, she could have expected from that somewhat academic quarter.

Finally, on the Saturday night, to her boundless astonishment and gratification, she received magnificent flowers and a note of warm congratulation from the Warrenders.

'Oscar Warrender!' exclaimed one of her fellow artists hanging over the flowers in admiration. 'Now we've seen everything! You couldn't very well have higher praise than that, could you?'

'No, I suppose one couldn't,' Gail agreed with a smile, 'Professionally,' she added, half to herself.

'What other praise would you want then?' The other

girl looked amused. 'What do you mean?'

'Oh, nothing,' Gail said quickly. For to no one could she admit how she longed and longed for that one word of praise from Marc which never came.

And when she was finally in the train on the Sunday morning, on the way to his home, she asked herself what madness had made her agree – no, actually *ask* – to go down there.

If she had had even a few minutes to think clearly on that crazy first night she would have withdrawn from the invitation. But it had been given and accepted, and then irrevocably sealed by the immediate departure of the elder Bannisters. And since then she had been unable to bring herself to telephone and cancel.

Could she have been sure that Mrs. Bannister would answer the telephone herself, Gail would have rung. But the thought that she might have to deal with a surprised Quentin Bannister or, still worse, Marc had prevented her. In weak indecision she had allowed the week to slip away, and now here she was – on the train.

At least Mrs. Bannister had said it would be she herself who would be meeting the train. Perhaps that would give one the very last-minute chance of withdrawing – of explaining that, of course, the idea was crude and ill-chosen. Mrs. Bannister would understand, Gail was almost certain. And then she could go back by the next train.

This excellent idea, however, had no chance of being put into practice. When Gail emerged from the country station, it was Marc who was standing by the car, holding the door open for her.

'Oh – oh, Marc, how nice to see you,' she said idiotically.

'Is it?' He smiled a little drily. 'I thought you might like a short drive around, as it's such a wonderful day.'

'That would be lovely,' she agreed despairingly, as he got into the driving seat beside her.

And they started off in a silence which seemed to Gail to rest on them like a tangible weight. She sought wildly in her mind for something which would fill the void. Some easy, conventional remark which could start them on a harmless round of conversation. But nothing came.

Presently, it was he who spoke. And he said quietly, 'There's no need to be so scared of me, Gail.'

'I'm not scared,' she asserted huskily. Then she had to swallow a great lump in her throat and to make tremendous efforts to hold back the tears which threatened to force their way under her lashes and down her cheeks in a humiliating trickle.

It was no good, however. A few did escape. And when he stopped the car with some stiff remark about the fine view he stared at her in dismay and exclaimed violently,

'For God's sake stop that! One would think you were expecting me to beat you or something. I'm not going to bully you or argue with you You're a perfectly free agent. You can sing in whatever you like and for whom you like. If you prefer Oliver to me—'

'But I don't! And stop shouting at me,' sobbed Gail. 'And I wish you'd turn the c-car and drive me straight back to the station. I'm c-catching the next train back to town.'

'You're doing nothing of the sort,' he said, and he took hold of her and gave her an angry, despairing sort of kiss which was no comfort to anyone. 'And what do you mean by saying you don't prefer Oliver to me? You were glad enough to be in his damned show, seemingly – and out of mine.'

'Of course I like Oliver and am glad to have helped him in his show. But do you suppose it wasn't a thousand times harder to refuse to sing for you than to agree to sing for him?'

'Hush!' he said suddenly, but with such authority that she stopped crying on a sort of shaming hiccup. 'Gail, I don't understand what you're talking about. Why did you have to refuse to sing in my opera?'

'Because Erna Spolianska was ten times better,' Gail said simply.

'But I wanted you. I *said* I wanted you.'

'It wasn't true, though.' Gail still spoke with that sort of desperate simplicity. 'You knew she was better than I was. You'd have been a fool if you'd thought otherwise. Only you had more or less promised the part to me, and you meant to stand by that. Your father knew too, in his heart. But his professional pride was involved in the fact that he'd backed me and trained me—'

'That too!' Marc exclaimed accusingly. 'How *could* you let my father use you to further his own confounded interference?'

'I wanted the part so much,' she said doggedly. 'I knew he was right when he said you wouldn't think much of me in the raw state. It was cheating, really, I suppose.' She sighed. 'What you heard and saw was not just me. It was the fine flower of your father's miraculous coaching. I know now it was an unpardonable thing to do. It meant that your father's idea of Anya was superimposed on me, so well that it shook your confidence in your own idea of your own character. But when you heard and saw that Polish girl, you *knew*. You thought it was too late – but you knew.'

'But,' he passed a hand over his hair in bewilderment, 'you say you did all this to get the part. Did violence to your better feelings, agreed to let Father more or less make a tool of you. And yet, when it came to the point, you left me flat and went off to Germany. It doesn't make sense.'

'Yes, it does really.' Gail drew another sigh, a rather unsteady one this time. 'At first I thought only about my own success. Though I was convinced it would be your success too. I couldn't imagine that your father wasn't right. But then – I began to have uneasy doubts. And finally – it always comes back to this – I saw Spolianska auditioned. And I knew she could be the making of your opera.'

'And, at that exact moment, you were offered this German contract?' he asked sceptically.

'No. Oscar Warrender got it for me.'

'God! I could wring his neck,' muttered Marc.

'No, you couldn't. His isn't the kind of neck one can wring,' stated Gail with spirit. 'Anyway he was right. He was the only one of the three of you who was looking at the issue dispassionately. He knew it had to be Spolianska. He was grudging about admitting it at first, until he found I was really in earnest. Then he said that if he'd written a work like "The Exile" and had the chance of an artist like Spolianska, he'd have committed murder to get her.'

'I'll still never forgive him.'

'Why not? Think back to that first night. Can you truly say, with all the artistic integrity you have, that he and I were wrong to force your hand?'

He was silent for almost a minute. Then he said, 'And are you asking me to believe it was artistic integrity which made *you* do all this?'

'Of course. I wanted the best for the opera.'

'Liar,' he said pleasantly. 'Why won't you tell me the

truth?' He leaned towards her, his eyes suddenly alight with amused triumph and joy. 'What was the reason, Gail?'

'I'm not going to say it first,' she cried rebelliously, and she hid her face against him. 'I've done my share of confessing.'

'Very well, ' he said, and he laughed with a tenderness she would not have believed possible. 'I love you, Gail. I adore you. My triumph was dust and ashes without you. Now what have you to say to me?'

'Just that – that I love you too. There's nothing else to say, because that's all that matters.'

'Oh, my darling—' he kissed her, very gently this time, 'that's all that matters. That we love each other and have found each other at last. When are you going to leave that show of Oliver's and marry me?'

'When the other girl is well enough to come back.'

'Not before then?'

'No. You wouldn't have me start by breaking faith with your family, would you?' She smiled up at him rather pertly.

He laughed, but he kissed her hard on her mouth.

'Will you promise to sing in an opera of mine one day?'

'If I'm better in the part than anyone else.'

'And who is going to be allowed to judge that, pray?'

'Oscar Warrender, I suppose. With perhaps,' Gail added reflectively, 'some assistance from your mother.'

'My mother!'

'Why not? I have an idea she knows more about this family than anyone else is ever likely to know.'

'Except you?' he suggested.

'Oh, I'm just a beginner,' declared Gail modestly.

'But you'll learn, my darling, you'll learn. For a first-year student, you haven't done badly already.' And he started the car and drove towards home with the air of a man who had found his heart's desire.

FREE!
Harlequin Romance Catalogue

Here is a wonderful opportunity to read many of the Harlequin Romances you may have missed.

The HARLEQUIN ROMANCE CATALOGUE lists hundreds of titles which possibly are no longer available at your local bookseller. To receive your copy, just fill out the coupon below, mail it to us, and we'll rush your catalogue to you!

Following this page you'll find a sampling of a few of the Harlequin Romances listed in the catalogue. Should you wish to order any of these immediately, kindly check the titles desired and mail with coupon.

Have You Missed Any of These
Harlequin Romances?

☐ 1009 NURSE AT FAIRCHILDS
    Marjorie Norrell
☐ 1011 THE TURQUOISE SEA
    Hilary Wilde
☐ 1013 MARY INTO MAIR
    Jane Ray
☐ 1017 ATTACHED TO DOCTOR
    MARCHMONT   Juliet Shore
☐ 1021 FOLLY TO BE WISE
    Sara Seale
☐ 1024 THE HOUSE OF DISCONTENT
    Esther Wyndham
☐ 1027 THE LONELY SHORE
    Anne Weale
☐ 1030 THE BLACK BENEDICTS
    Anita Charles
☐ 1076 BELLS IN THE WIND
    Kate Starr
☐ 1100 THE BROKEN WING
    Mary Burchell
☐ 1108 SUMMER EVERY DAY
    Jane Arbor
☐ 1145 YOUNG DOCTOR YERDLEY
    Anne Durham
☐ 1173 RED AS A ROSE
    Hilary Wilde
☐ 1184 THE HOUSE OF OLIVER
    Jean S. Macleod
☐ 1199 JOHNNY NEXT DOOR
    Margaret Malcolm
☐ 1227 A MAN APART
    Jane Donnelly
☐ 1231 IMITATION MARRIAGE
    Phyllis Matthewman
☐ 1234 DESERT GOLD
    Pamela Kent
☐ 1249 DOCTOR ARNOLD'S AMBITION
    Pauline Ash
☐ 1254 THE MASTER OF KEILLS
    Jean S Macleod
☐ 1257 DOCTOR AT VILLA RONDA
    Iris Danbury
☐ 1270 THOUGH WORLDS APART
    Mary Burchell
☐ 1277 STRANGER'S TRESPASS
    Jane Arbor
☐ 1280 THE FLIGHT OF THE SWAN
    Eleanor Farnes
☐ 1290 A SUMMER TO LOVE
    Roumelia Lane

☐ 1291 MASTER OF GLENKEITH
    Jean S. Macleod
☐ 1294 THE BREADTH OF HEAVEN
    Rosemary Pollock
☐ 1296 THE WIND AND THE SPRAY
    Joyce Dingwell
☐ 1299 THE LISTENING PALMS
    Juliet Shore
☐ 1303 STILL WATERS
    Marguerite Lees
☐ 1305 DOCTOR GEYER'S PROJECT
    Marjorie Norrell
☐ 1306 A HANDFUL OF SILVER
    Isobel Chace
☐ 1310 TAWNY ARE THE LEAVES
    Wynne May
☐ 1315 WHERE THE KOWHAI BLOOMS
    Mary Moore
☐ 1320 SPANISH LACE
    Joyce Dingwell
☐ 1325 NO SOONER LOVED
    Pauline Garner
☐ 1331 HOTEL BELVEDERE
    Iris Danbury
☐ 1337 THE CAMPBELLS ARE COMING
    Felicity Hayle
☐ 1344 THE DANGEROUS DELIGHT
    Violet Winspear
☐ 1352 THE MOUNTAIN OF STARS
    Catherine Airlie
☐ 1357 RIPPLES IN THE LAKE
    Mary Coates
☐ 1361 SISTER PETERS IN
    AMSTERDAM   Betty Neels
☐ 1367 INTERLUDE IN ARCADY
    Margery Hilton
☐ 1370 THE WAYS OF LOVE
    Catherine Airlie
☐ 1374 FORTUNE'S LEAD
    Barbara Perkins
☐ 1380 RELUCTANT MASQUERADE
    Henrietta Reid
☐ 1389 MAN OF THE FOREST
    Hilda Pressley
☐ 1396 BRIGHT WILDERNESS
    Gwen Westwood
☐ 1400 THE DISTANT TRAP
    Gloria Bevan
☐ 1404 DIAMONDS ON THE LAKE
    Mary Cummins

All books are 50c.   Please use the handy order coupon.

Have You Missed Any of These
Harlequin Romances?

☐ 1010 DOCTOR OF RESEARCH
   Elizabeth Houghton
☐ 1014 HOUSE OF LORRAINE
   Rachel Lindsay
☐ 1019 FLOWER OF THE MORNING
   Celine Conway
☐ 1022 YOUNG ELLIS Margery Hilton
☐ 1025 SURGERY IN THE HILLS
   Ivy Ferrari
☐ 1028 THE MASTER OF
   NORMANHURST
   Margaret Malcolm
☐ 1031 FLOWERING DESERT
   Elizabeth Hoy
☐ 1134 THE MAN WHO CAME BACK
   Pamela Kent
☐ 1148 FLOWERING WILDERNESS
   Kathryn Blair
☐ 1149 A NIGHTINGALE IN THE
   SYCAMORE   J. Beaufort
☐ 1154 YOU CAN'T STAY HERE
   Barbara Gilmour
☐ 1164 MEADOWSWEET
   Margaret Malcolm
☐ 1171 THE WINGS OF MEMORY
   Eleanor Farnes
☐ 1181 DANGEROUS LOVE
   Jane Beaufort
☐ 1182 GOLDEN APPLE ISLAND
   Jane Arbor
☐ 1206 SUBSTITUTE FOR LOVE
   Henrietta Reid
☐ 1214 THE MARSHALL FAMILY
   Mary Burchell
☐ 1215 SOFT IS THE MUSIC
   Jane Beech
☐ 1228 THE YOUNG NIGHTINGALES
   Mary Whistler
☐ 1229 A TASTE FOR LOVE
   Joyce Dingwell
☐ 1230 CROWN OF CONTENT
   Janice Gray
☐ 1235 LOVE AS IT FLIES
   Marguerite Lees
☐ 1243 THE ISLE OF SONG
   Hilary Wilde
☐ 1246 THE CONSTANT HEART
   Eleanor Farnes
☐ 1253 DREAM COME TRUE
   Patricia Fenwick

☐ 1261 WITH ALL MY HEART
   Nan Asquith
☐ 1274 MAN FROM THE SEA
   Pamela Kent
☐ 1285 OUT OF A DREAM
   Jean Curtis
☐ 1293 I KNOW MY LOVE
   Sara Seale
☐ 1297 DENTAL NURSE AT DENLEY'S
   Marjorie Lewty
☐ 1301 HOTEL BY THE LOCH
   Iris Danbury
☐ 1304 SHARLIE FOR SHORT
   Dorothy Rivers
☐ 1307 A CHANCE TO WIN
   Margaret Rome
☐ 1311 THE MARRIAGE WHEEL
   Susan Barrie
☐ 1316 CAN THIS BE LOVE ?
   Margaret Malcolm
☐ 1322 WIND THROUGH THE
   VINEYARDS   J. Armstrong
☐ 1327 MORE THAN GOLD
   Hilda Pressley
☐ 1332 DON'T WALK ALONE
   Jane Donelly
☐ 1338 SEA OF ZANJ Roumelia Lane
☐ 1346 A HOUSE CALLED KANGAROO
   Gladys Fullbrook
☐ 1355 RISING STAR
   Kay Thorpe
☐ 1358 HOME TO WHITE WINGS
   Jean Dunbar
☐ 1363 STAR DUST
   Margaret Malcolm
☐ 1368 MUSIC I HEARD WITH YOU
   Elizabeth Hoy
☐ 1371 DANCING ON MY HEART
   Belinda Dell
☐ 1376 SHADOWS FROM THE SEA
   Jane Donnelly
☐ 1382 TO JOURNEY TOGETHER
   Mary Burchell
☐ 1392 THAT YOUNG PERSON
   Sara Seale
☐ 1397 IF LOVE WERE WISE
   Elizabeth Hoy
☐ 1401 ONE STRING FOR NURSE
   BOW   Joyce Dingwell
☐ 1405 THE CURTAIN RISES
   Mary Burchell

Have You Missed Any of These
Harlequin Romances?

☐ 1075 CINDERELLA AFTER
MIDNIGHT   Mary Burchell
☐ 1104 THE FAITHLESS ONE
Elizabeth Hoy
☐ 1128 THE QUIET HEART
Susan Barrie
☐ 1130 DALTON'S DAUGHTER
Kate Starr
☐ 1132 DARK HORSE, DARK RIDER
Elizabeth Hoy
☐ 1140 THE MAN IN HOMESPUN
Margaret Malcolm
☐ 1144 THE TRUANT BRIDE
Sara Seale
☐ 1152 A GARLAND OF MARIGOLDS
Isobel Chace
☐ 1162 ISLAND OF LOVE
Belinda Dell
☐ 1163 LOVE IN THE WILDERNESS
Dorothy Rivers
☐ 1165 WARD OF LUCIFER
Mary Burchell
☐ 1167 DEAR BARBARIAN
Janice Gray
☐ 1168 ROSE IN THE BUD
Susan Barrie
☐ 1171 THE WINGS OF MEMORY
Eleanor Farnes
☐ 1173 RED AS A ROSE
Hilary Wilde
☐ 1176 WINDS OF ENCHANTMENT
Rosalind Brett
☐ 1180 ROSE OF THE DESERT
Roumelia Lane
☐ 1186 SOMEONE ELSE'S HEART
Barbara Allen
☐ 1188 THE GROTTO OF JADE
Margery Hilton
☐ 1190 THE SHADOW AND THE SUN
Amanda Doyle
☐ 1192 THE CERTAIN SPRING
Nan Asquith
☐ 1194 SUNSHINE YELLOW
Mary Whistler
☐ 1195 SPREAD YOUR WINGS
Ruth Clemence
☐ 1197 PENNY PLAIN
Sara Seale
☐ 1202 LAND OF HEART'S DESIRE
Catherine Airlie

☐ 1203 THE LUCKY ONE
Marjorie Lewty
☐ 1205 THE SUN AND THE SEA
Marguerite Lees
☐ 1210 A FRIEND OF THE FAMILY
Hilda Nickson
☐ 1211 BRIDE OF KILSAIG
Iris Danbury
☐ 1226 HONEYMOON HOLIDAY
Elizabeth Hoy
☐ 1234 DESERT GOLD
Pamela Kent
☐ 1237 THE LAST OF THE
MALLORY'S   Kay Thorpe
☐ 1239 THIS WISH I HAVE
Amanda Doyle
☐ 1240 THE GREEN RUSHES
Catherine Airlie
☐ 1241 NURSE BARLOW'S JINX
Marjorie Norrell
☐ 1249 DOCTOR ARNOLD'S AMBITION
Pauline Ash
☐ 1251 VENICE AFFAIR
Joyce Dingwell
☐ 1266 WHERE NO STARS SHINE
Ivy Ferrari
☐ 1275 SHAKE OUT THE STARS
Janice Gray
☐ 1282 THE SHINING STAR
Hilary Wilde
☐ 1284 ONLY MY HEART TO GIVE
Nan Asquith
☐ 1288 THE LAST OF THE KINTYRES
Catherine Airlie
☐ 1381 MUSIC ON THE WIND
Dorothy Slide
☐ 1383 A WIFE FOR ANDREW
Lucy Gillen
☐ 1385 NURSE IN HOLLAND
Betty Neels
☐ 1388 UNWARY HEART
Anne Hampson
☐ 1390 SUGAR IN THE MORNING
Isobel Chace
☐ 1391 MY VALIANT FLEDGLING
Margaret Malcolm
☐ 1392 THAT YOUNG PERSON
Sara Seale
☐ 1399 BLUE JASMINE
Violet Winspear

All books are 50c.   Please use the handy order coupon.

Have You Missed Any of These
Harlequin Romances?

- ☐ 1103 HEART OF GOLD
  Marjorie Moore
- ☐ 1106 WELCOME TO PARADISE
  Jill Tahourdin
- ☐ 1126 MAN OF THE ISLANDS
  Henrietta Reid
- ☐ 1129 MY FRIEND, DOCTOR JOHN
  Marjorie Norrell
- ☐ 1138 LOVING IS GIVING
  Mary Burchell
- ☐ 1142 SECRET HEIRESS
  Eleanor Farnes
- ☐ 1146 THE IMPERFECT SECRETARY
  Marjorie Lewty
- ☐ 1150 THE BRIDE OF MINGALAY
  Jean S. Macleod
- ☐ 1153 THE RETURN OF SISTER
  BARNETT   E. Houghton
- ☐ 1212 HIDEAWAY HEART
  Roumelia Lane
- ☐ 1236 JEMIMA
  Leonora Starr
- ☐ 1247 LAIRD OF STORR
  Henrietta Reid
- ☐ 1281 NURSE SALLY'S LAST
  CHANCE   Anne Durham
- ☐ 1283 ROSALIND COMES HOME
  Essie Summers
- ☐ 1287 THE WALLED GARDEN
  Margaret Malcolm
- ☐ 1314 SUMMER ISLAND
  Jean S. Macleod
- ☐ 1317 BELOVED SPARROW
  Henrietta Reid
- ☐ 1319 BRITTLE BONDAGE
  Rosalind Brett
- ☐ 1321 BUSH HOSPITAL
  Gladys Fullbrook
- ☐ 1324 QUEEN OF HEARTS
  Sara Seale
- ☐ 1326 MEET ON MY GROUND
  Essie Summers
- ☐ 1328 A WIND SIGHING
  Catherine Airlie
- ☐ 1330 A HOME FOR JOY
  Mary Burchell
- ☐ 1333 KEEPER OF THE HEART
  Gwen Westwood
- ☐ 1336 THE CYPRESS GARDEN
  Jane Arbor

- ☐ 1339 SLAVE OF THE WIND
  Jean S. Macleod
- ☐ 1341 FIRE IS FOR SHARING
  Doris E. Smith
- ☐ 1342 THE FEEL OF SILK
  Joyce Dingwell
- ☐ 1345 THREE NURSES
  Louise Ellis
- ☐ 1347 THE TRUANT SPIRIT
  Sara Seale
- ☐ 1348 REVOLT, AND VIRGINIA
  Essie Summers
- ☐ 1354 WHEN LOVE'S BEGINNING
  Mary Burchell
- ☐ 1359 RETURN TO TREMARTH
  Susan Barrie
- ☐ 1362 STRANGER BY MY SIDE
  Jeannette Welsh
- ☐ 1366 DESIGN FOR LOVING
  Margaret Baumann
- ☐ 1372 ISLE OF POMEGRANATES
  Iris Danbury
- ☐ 1375 THE KINDLED FIRE
  Essie Summers
- ☐ 1395 TERMINUS TEHRAN
  Roumelia Lane
- ☐ 1403 WHISPER TO THE STARS
  Hettie Grimstead
- ☐ 1406 WALK INTO THE WIND
  Jane Arbor
- ☐ 1407 NEXT STOP GRETNA
  Belinda Dell
- ☐ 1410 NURSE DEBORAH
  Marjorie Norrell
- ☐ 1411 TURN THE PAGE
  Nan Asquith
- ☐ 1412 JOURNEY OF ENCHANTMENT
  Gladys Fullbrook
- ☐ 1553 DOCTOR TOBY
  Lucy Gillen
- ☐ 1554 THE KEYS OF THE CASTLE
  Barbara Rowan
- ☐ 1555 RAINTREE VALLEY
  Violet Winspear
- ☐ 1556 NO ENEMY
  Hilda Nickson
- ☐ 1557 ALONG THE RIBBONWOOD
  TRACK   Mary Moore
- ☐ 1558 LEGEND OF ROSCANO
  Iris Danbury

All books are 50c. Please use the handy order coupon.

A